Sloan had nothing to offer her

She was a client, nothing more. When this was over, Rachel and her son would go back to their lives. And Sloan...well, he would return to his usual existence.

He watched Rachel trudge across the courtyard. She looked beat. She couldn't have had more than two hours' sleep last night.

Sloan caught himself. He would not feel any sympathy. No way. He had to rebuild that mutual dislike that had first stood between them.

When he was sure Rachel had retired to her own room, he finally went inside. The house was quiet. No sweet, feminine laughter. No pitter-patter of little feet. Already he missed the kid's questions, and Rachel's singsong voice as she played with her son. This wasn't supposed to happen.

He had sworn that no one would ever get this close to him again.

Dear Harlequin Intrigue Reader,

Welcome to a brand-new year of exciting romance and edge-of-your-seat suspense. We at Harlequin Intrigue are thrilled to renew our commitment to you, our loyal readers, to provide variety and outstanding romantic suspense—each and every month.

To get things started right, veteran Harlequin Intrigue author Cassie Miles kicks off a two-book miniseries with *State of Emergency*. The COLORADO SEARCH AND RESCUE group features tough emergency personnel reared in the shadows of the rugged Rocky Mountains. Who wouldn't want to be stranded with a western-born hunk trained to protect and serve?

Speaking of hunks, Debra Webb serves up a giant of a man in *Solitary Soldier*, the next installment in her COLBY AGENCY series. And you know what they say about the bigger they come the harder they fall.... Well, it goes double for this wounded hero.

Ann Voss Peterson takes us to the darkest part of a serial killer's world in *Accessory to Marriage*. The second time around could prove to be the last—permanently— for both the hero and heroine in this gripping thriller.

Finally, please welcome Delores Fossen to the line. She joins us with a moving story of forced artificial insemination, which unites two strangers who unwittingly become parents...and eventually a family. Do not miss *His Child* for an emotional read.

Be sure to let us know how we're doing; we love to hear from our readers! And Happy New Year from all of us at Harlequin Intrigue.

Sincerely,

Denise O'Sullivan
Associate Senior Editor
Harlequin Intrigue

SOLITARY SOLDIER
DEBRA WEBB

TORONTO · NEW YORK · LONDON
AMSTERDAM · PARIS · SYDNEY · HAMBURG
STOCKHOLM · ATHENS · TOKYO · MILAN · MADRID
PRAGUE · WARSAW · BUDAPEST · AUCKLAND

ISBN 0-373-22646-2

SOLITARY SOLDIER

Copyright © 2002 by Debra Webb

Visit us at www.eHarlequin.com

Printed in U.S.A.

ABOUT THE AUTHOR

Debra Webb was born in Scottsboro, Alabama, to parents who taught her that anything is possible if you want it badly enough. She began writing at age nine. Eventually, she met and married the man of her dreams and tried some other occupations, including selling vacuum cleaners, working in a factory, a day care center, a hospital and a department store. When her husband joined the military, they moved to Berlin, Germany, and Debra became a secretary in the commanding general's office. By 1985 they were back in the States, and finally moved to Tennessee, to a small town where everyone knows everyone else. With the support of her husband and two beautiful daughters, Debra took up writing again, looking to mystery and movies for inspiration. In 1998 her dream of writing for Harlequin came true. You can write to Debra with your comments at P.O. Box 64, Huntland, Tennessee 37345.

Books by Debra Webb

HARLEQUIN INTRIGUE
583—SAFE BY HIS SIDE*
597—THE BODYGUARD'S BABY*
610—PROTECTIVE CUSTODY*
634—SPECIAL ASSIGNMENT: BABY
646—SOLITARY SOLDIER*

*Colby Agency

HARLEQUIN AMERICAN ROMANCE
864—LONGWALKER'S CHILD

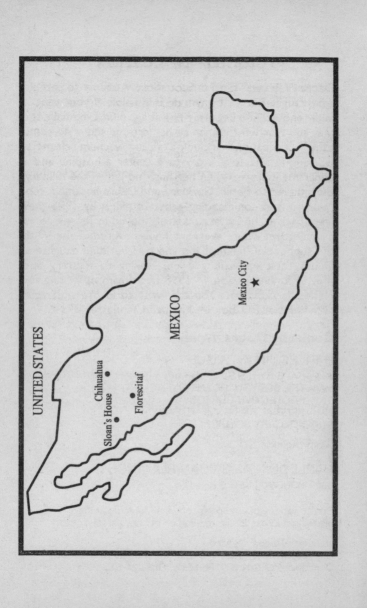

CAST OF CHARACTERS

Rachel Larson—She cannot allow Angel to get his hands on her son. She will do whatever it takes to protect the child from his father.

Trevor Sloan—The last thing he wants or needs is a woman and a child reminding him of all he has lost.

Josh—Rachel's four-year-old son. Can she protect him from his own father?

Gabriel DiCassi, aka "Angel"—A highly paid assassin. He wants his son and he will stop at nothing to get him.

Victoria Colby—The head of the Colby Agency. She sends Rachel and her son to Sloan. Despite Sloan's mercenary mentality, Victoria knows that he is Rachel's only hope.

Tanya—Angel's longtime lover. She wants Angel all to herself, but can she risk his wrath to accomplish her heart's desire?

Ric Martinez—Colby Agency's newest field operative. He has attitude and charm, necessary skills to get the information he needs to fulfill his mission.

First, I must thank Greyhound bus lines
for the ride of our lives, and God
for providing the snow that trapped us in Cleveland
on our way to New York. Had I not been stuck on a bus
with my partner-in-crime for thirty-one hours,
this story might not have been born.

This book is dedicated to a dear friend
and fellow writer. She is my partner-in-crime,
just as Ethel was to Lucy. We began this journey
together—may it always be as fun, exciting and "bizarre"
as it was in the beginning when we couldn't wait for
"the call." Cheers, Rhonda, we made it.

Prologue

"I'll pay anything you ask," Rachel Larson insisted.

Victoria Colby regarded the woman across the wide expanse of her oak desk for a long moment before she responded. "Miss Larson, this is primarily an investigations agency. We accept clients who require personal protection on a case-by-case basis, and generally by referral only."

Disappointment shadowed Rachel's pale features. Dark circles beneath eyes that contained as much wariness as fear, and the ill fit of her clothing told Victoria that this young woman had not slept or eaten well in too many months. Her overall look of extreme fatigue signaled her proximity to the edge. The ability to size up a client had facilitated Victoria's climb to the top in this business. And right now, every instinct told her that this young woman was more than simply desperate.

"I'll need to know a great deal more before I can make a decision as to whether the Colby Agency will take your case," Victoria explained.

Rachel drew in a shaky breath and squared her shoulders. "Detective Clarence Taylor sent me. He was a police detective here in Chicago before moving to New Orleans.''

Victoria considered the name for a moment. "Yes, I remember Detective Taylor. He left three or four years ago I believe.''

Rachel nodded, hope kindled in those dark brown eyes. ''That's right. He knows that I've exhausted every other possibility, including the police.'' Rachel leaned forward and clutched Victoria's desk like a lifeline against the violent waters churning her obviously troubled soul. ''You have to help me, Mrs. Colby. He's going to take my little boy.'' A single tear slipped down her colorless cheek before she could swipe it away with the back of her hand. ''I can't let him do that.''

Sympathy tugged at Victoria's softer side—the side that hadn't hardened over the years in this cutthroat business. She knew all too well that kind of fear, that kind of pain. She blocked the memories. If Clarence Taylor had sent Miss Larson to her, Victoria would certainly do all she could to help her. ''All right,'' she offered. ''I will consider your case, but you have to tell me *everything*, Miss Larson.''

''Thank you.'' Rachel's voice cracked with emotion.

Victoria opened her notepad and removed her gold pen from its holder. ''I'll need to know as many details as possible about the stalker.'' She glanced up from her pad. ''First, do you know his name?''

Rachel licked her lips, then swallowed visibly. ''I believe your agency has worked on a case involving him before. His name is Gabriel DiCassi. They call him—''

''Angel,'' Victoria finished for her, the name barely more than a whisper. She shuddered with remembered dread. Several years, but not nearly enough, had passed since she heard that name. Not since...Sloan left.

"Detective Taylor thought that one of your investigators might have experience dealing with...him," she said uncertainly.

Taking her time, Victoria placed her pen on the blank notepad, then leveled her gaze on Rachel's. "Unfortunately, I do know him."

Despair reigned supreme in the young woman's features. "Then you know that this is no ordinary situation."

"Yes," Victoria agreed gravely. "Angel is a highly paid assassin whose reputation boasts a perfect record of kills. He's ruthless. If you're his target, he won't stop until you're dead."

"Please tell me you'll help me." Desperation weighed Rachel's weary tone. "I have to find a way to protect my son."

A frown tugged at Victoria. Somehow the part about the child didn't quite gel. "Why would Angel want to take your son?" Victoria thought briefly of the small dark-haired boy sitting in her outer office under her secretary Mildred's watchful eye.

Rachel looked away for a moment. "Because he's Josh's father." Her lips trembled with the effort it took to force her next words. "Five years ago, we were...involved."

"Involved?" Victoria heard the contempt in her own voice, and immediately regretted it. Humiliation clouded Rachel's expression.

"I was very young. It was a mistake." She squeezed her eyes shut and shook her head slowly from side to side. A soul-deep pain clouded her gaze when she opened her eyes once more. "He used me to get to my father."

"Yet you're still alive." Victoria arched a speculative brow. "That's not Angel's style. He never leaves loose ends."

"He would have killed me..." Rachel blinked furiously at the tears gathering, then shrugged. "I was lucky to escape. I've been running ever since. Later, he found out about Josh, and now Angel wants him."

If her story were true, Rachel Larson was as good as dead. Angel allowed nothing to stand between him and what he wanted. Anyone who tried to stop him was accepting a death sentence. Though Victoria employed the very finest in their fields, tracking down a man like Angel would take resources she simply could not risk. She had learned that lesson too well seven years ago.

Victoria braced herself for what she knew had to be said. "Regrettably, Miss Larson, the Colby Agency cannot provide the services you have requested."

Rachel stiffened. "You won't help me?"

"I don't mean that at all." Victoria pulled open her right desk drawer and flipped through her files. She removed a manila folder and scanned its contents. Satisfied with what she found, Victoria turned her attention back to Rachel. "There is only one man, to my knowledge, who knows Angel well enough to be of any assistance to you, and he doesn't work for me anymore." Victoria copied the name and address from the folder onto the back of her business card. "I can't guarantee that he'll be willing to take your case, but he's your only possible hope at succeeding. Tell him I sent you."

Rachel accepted the offered card. "Who is he?"

"Someone who used to work for this agency." Victoria leveled her gaze on Rachel's. "Someone I would trust with my own life. His name is Trevor Sloan."

"He must be the investigator Detective Taylor mentioned."

Victoria dipped her head in acknowledgment. "Sloan was the best investigator the Colby Agency has ever had the privilege of employing." Regret trickled through her. "As I said, he doesn't work for me anymore. Although this agency has utilized his services from time to time over the past couple of years, Sloan is very selective in the offers he takes these days." Victoria paused before continuing. "Considering the circumstances, he might not want to take your case at all."

Rachel searched Victoria's gaze. "If he's willing, how can he help me?"

Memories Victoria would rather not have recalled played in the private theater of her mind. "He knows Angel. He knows how the man operates and what motivates him."

Frowning, Rachel hesitated at first, but then asked, "How is it that Sloan knows Angel so well?"

Victoria sighed her own hesitation. What would it hurt to tell her? If Sloan could help the woman, Victoria rationalized, understanding would make dealing with him somewhat easier. "Seven years ago Angel assassinated two very prominent businessmen here in Chicago," she began. "The Colby Agency was called in to consult on the case." Victoria tamped down the guilt that quickly surfaced. "I assigned Sloan to support them. He possesses an uncanny ability to read people. He studied Angel's case, tracked him for months." Victoria met Rachel's unsuspecting gaze knowing that what she would say next would only add to her growing fear. "When Sloan got too close, Angel retaliated in a particularly ruthless manner. Recognizing the kind of man Sloan was and what would hurt him most, Angel murdered Sloan's wife and took his three-year-old son."

Rachel gasped and her eyes widened in horror. "Oh God."

"The child's body wasn't discovered for a while, and during that time Angel taunted Sloan with telephone calls of his son's recorded cries for Daddy..." Her voice drifted off as the painful memories of that seemingly endless year of tracking Angel sifted through Victoria's thoughts. Sloan had pushed himself beyond any man's physical and mental limitations, and found nothing. Then, finally, they'd discovered the small body burned beyond recognition. Something had snapped inside Sloan then and he'd simply disappeared. Months later, Victoria learned that he'd resurfaced as a private contractor in Mexico. He hadn't allowed her close since. But he was still the best in the business of tracking and protection.

Rachel's complexion turned a whiter shade of pale. "How will I ever stop him?"

Victoria studied her a long moment before answering. Perhaps Angel had some sort of twisted reasoning for allowing Rachel to live just as he had when he spared Sloan's life. Living with the loss was much more difficult than dying. Gabriel DiCassi was evil incarnate.

Victoria pointed to the card in Rachel's hand. "Talk to Sloan." If even a small part of the man she once knew lived behind that hardened, go-to-hell armor he wore, Sloan would never be able to turn this woman and her child away. And maybe the opportunity would allow him to lay his own demons to rest. "And don't let his attitude scare you off," Victoria added. "If there is anyone who can help you, Sloan can."

RACHEL STOOD ON the street corner in downtown Chicago and stared at the card in her hand. Los Laureles Cantina in Florescitaf, Mexico. That's where she would find this man named Sloan. What sort of man used a cantina for his business office? Maybe she didn't want to know. Rachel shivered despite the August sun beating down from the clear blue sky. No amount of heat would ever make her feel warm inside knowing what lay ahead of her.

But she had no choice…she had to do something.

No matter how far and fast she ran, Angel always found her. He wanted her son. Angel only allowed her to take care of Josh for the time being because he felt the boy needed his mother. He had said those very words to her on more than one occasion. One day though, he intended to take Josh. Rachel shuddered at the thought. She had to do something before that day came.

"I'm hungry, Mommy."

Rachel's attention jerked back to the here and now. She smiled at the little boy whose hand she held tightly in her own. "I'm sorry, honey. We'll have lunch soon." Satisfied, Josh smiled back at her. Somehow she had to find Sloan and convince him to help her.

No matter what it took.

Chapter One

Thank God.

After searching all afternoon beneath the blistering August sun, Rachel Larson had finally found the place no one seemed to know about. Or perhaps it was her poor excuse for Spanish they didn't understand. Rachel surveyed the run-down building before her. Located in an unsavory part of an obscure little Mexican town called Florescitaf, the cantina known as Los Laureles looked even more forbidding than she had expected. Maybe that's why no one would admit to knowing its location.

Squaring her shoulders against the uneasiness skittering up her spine, Rachel reminded herself of why she was here. She had to do this. There was no other alternative. Besides, the place was named after some sort of flower, surely it couldn't be so bad.

Instinctively Rachel tightened her hold on Josh's hand when he peeked around her skirt to watch the children playing in the alley between the cantina and the equally run-down, open-air meat market next door. Rachel glanced down at her son and smiled when his eyes widened in wonder at the goats the children appeared to be tending. Barefoot, and faces bright with smiles, the local children stared back at Josh with that same wonder in their dark eyes.

Josh seldom played with other children. They were never in one place long enough to make friends, and even if they were, ties to anyone was just another risk Rachel and Josh couldn't afford. Rachel sighed. Would their lives never be normal?

Rachel stole one last, lingering moment to savor the children's innocent faces, the warmth of the merciless sun, and the pungent smells of raw, drying and roasting meat from the nearby market. After today, one way or another, her life would never be the same.

Today things were going to change.

Drawing in a deep, bolstering breath, Rachel took the first step toward that end. The stench of stale tobacco, alcohol and sweat enveloped her as she entered the disreputable-looking cantina. Overhead ancient fans slowly stirred the fetid air. Before her eyes adjusted to the dim, smoky interior, Rachel felt one narrowed gaze after the other scrutinize her as if she were the latest addition to the menu. Uncertainty warred with the desperation that was her constant companion.

You can do this, Rach, she reminded the part of her that wanted to run as far away from here as possible. Angel had warned her that he was growing impatient with her useless measures to elude him. What would he do when he discovered that she had come to this man named Sloan? Rachel shivered, and pushed away the thought. She couldn't think about that now.

This was the only way.

Still holding Josh's hand in her left and with her right clenched tightly around the strap of her over-stuffed shoulder bag, Rachel weaved her way between the tables and to the bar that extended half the length of the room. She hated to bring her four-year-old son into a place like this, but what else could she do? She didn't dare allow him out of her sight. And she had to find Sloan.

Their lives depended upon it.

"Excuse me," Rachel said as politely as possible with fear pounding through her veins. "Do you speak English?"

"*Sí.* What is your pleasure, *señora?*" Propped against the worn smooth counter, the bartender's examining gaze lingered on Rachel's breasts before he looked up and smiled.

Heavyset, with thick dark hair and a wide mustache, the man oozed what he likely considered charm. Rachel swallowed the fear clawing at her throat and manufactured a tight smile of her own. "I'm looking for a man called Sloan."

One bushy eyebrow quirked the slightest bit, but the smile stayed in place. "And why would such a pretty lady look for such a dangerous man?" he asked in that heavily accented voice, putting emphasis on the words *pretty lady*.

"A friend sent me." What if he wouldn't tell her where Sloan was? What if Sloan wasn't even here? He could be working some other case in God knows where. What would she do then? Rachel's heart pounded so hard she felt sure the man behind the counter could hear it.

"It's very important that I find him," she forged ahead, her voice faltering despite her best efforts to keep it firm. Rachel moistened her lips and held her ground as he took his time considering her request.

"*El solitario.*" With a jerk of his head, the bartender

gestured toward the darkest corner of the establishment. "The one who sits all alone."

Rachel nodded stiffly. "Thank you."

Before she could turn, his next words stopped her. "Do not thank me, *señora*. It is not my habit to send sheep to slaughter, but you asked." He picked up a grimy cloth and absently wiped the counter, his gaze still leveled on hers.

Rachel stared at him, uncertain what to do with his offhanded warning. Should she run now and cut her losses? Her hand tightened around Josh's. Maybe Victoria had been wrong about Sloan.

"It's very important."

The bartender shrugged. "Perhaps, pretty lady, you should come back later." He darted a look at the faded plastic clock on the wall. "It is just four o'clock, his mood will be nasty for a while yet."

"I'll…" Rachel backed up a step. "Thank you," she said hesitantly. She glanced down at Josh and said another quick prayer before starting in the direction the bartender had indicated. Surely the bartender was exaggerating. Sloan couldn't be as fearsome as all that. Victoria Colby had recommended him. He was a former employee of hers. The Colby Agency had come highly recommended to Rachel. She trusted Detective Taylor's judgment implicitly.

Ignoring what were most likely lewd Spanish remarks tossed in her direction, Rachel walked straight to the far end of the room. She would show no fear. She was not afraid, she chanted like a mantra with each step she took. Rachel paused a few feet away from her destination and pulled out a chair from an unoccupied table. After settling Josh into the seat, she crouched in front of him and forced a wide smile she didn't in any way feel.

"Josh, I want you to stay right here until Mommy speaks to the man just over there." Rachel pointed out the table only a few feet away. "Okay, sweetie?"

Josh bobbed his head up and down, his eyes wide with uncertainty, and even a little fear. Rachel's heart squeezed in her chest. Josh would start school next year. How many of his classmates will have experienced a place such as this? Then again, how many of them could claim the devil himself as a father?

Rachel pushed aside the painful thoughts and ruffled her son's dark hair. She pulled a coloring book and small box of crayons from her bag and placed them on the scarred tabletop. "I want you to color Mommy a pretty picture and I'll only be a minute."

Josh nodded once and flipped the coloring book to a fresh page. Satisfied, Rachel stood. She forced herself to turn away from the child she loved more than life itself. She looked back twice as she took the few remaining steps, each time hoping to comfort Josh with the halfhearted smile her trembling lips managed to maintain.

Her son waved shyly and Rachel felt a real smile spread across her lips then. Yes, she could do this. She would do it for Josh. Confident in her decision, Rachel turned back to her objective.

The man sat alone, an empty tequila bottle on the table before him. *El solitario* reverberated through Rachel. A solitary soldier. A mercenary for hire. Just the kind of man she needed. He didn't look up when she stopped an arm's length away. He seemed fascinated with the gold liquid in the glass he was turning between his thumb and forefinger.

Rachel's first up-close impression of the man was *dangerous,* just like the bartender said. Sloan looked like he would be tall, and he was definitely solidly built. His too-long tawny hair brushed his broad shoulders. The sleeves had been cut from the faded shirt he wore, displaying muscled arms. He looked very strong, and for one fleeting moment Rachel felt a little safer in the knowledge that this was the man who could help her.

But then he spoke...

"Unless you're selling your wares, I'm not interested."

Rachel shivered at the husky sound of his deep voice. Disregarding his crude remark, she summoned her waning courage and asked, "Are you Sloan?"

He lifted his gaze to hers then, and Rachel's breath caught. Icy, translucent blue eyes cut a hole straight to her soul. His square, beard-shadowed jaw reaffirmed her first impression. *Dangerous.*

"Unfortunately—" He tossed back the last of the tequila in his glass without taking that piercing gaze from hers. Rachel jumped when the glass clunked down onto the table. "—I haven't had enough to drink to be anyone else." He licked the taste of liquor from his lips. "But it's still early."

Mustering her scattered courage, Rachel forced herself to speak. "I've come a long way and—"

"You do know," he interrupted as if she hadn't spoken at all, "that this is no place for children." His gaze darted past her to where she had left her son.

Rachel glanced over her shoulder to make sure Josh was okay. She swallowed back the mushrooming uncertainty. "I know," she replied slowly, her resolve crumbling beneath his stony, emotionless glare. "My name is Rachel Larson. I...I need your help."

In one fluid motion he stood and towered over her. She battled the urge to flee. Absolute silence screamed around them for the space of two heartbeats before he responded.

"Then you've wasted your time, Miss Larson."

Her heart lurched. "Please, you have to hear me out."

One side of his mouth quirked upward. "The only thing I have to do is die. And between now and then, all I plan to do is drink tequila and get laid. Anything else is uncertain." He cocked his head and made a sound, more growl than laugh. "So unless you plan to help me with one of those two things, I would suggest that you don't waste any more of your time or mine."

A new surge of fear shot through Rachel's veins. She could not allow him to dismiss her so easily. He was her only chance. "Victoria Colby sent me," Rachel announced in a stronger voice than she had thought herself capable. "She said you could help me."

Something flickered in that cold, remote gaze, then vanished as quickly as it came. "Victoria made a mistake."

Before Rachel could protest, he turned and started toward the bar, his smooth stride unhurried and making her think of a panther as it stalked its prey.

Watching her only hope slip through her fingers, desperation tightened Rachel's chest. She had to do or say something to convince him to help her.

Now!

"Angel intends to kill me," she blurted. "If you won't help me, what am I supposed to do?"

Sloan stopped and turned to face her. He stared at

Rachel for a long moment with those pale, empty eyes, his unrevealing expression unchanged. What felt like a lifetime later, he spoke, "Get your affairs in order."

Stunned by his indifference, and frightened beyond reason by his refusal, Rachel watched him walk to the bar and order another drink. The bartender filled a clean glass with tequila, the sound echoing around her, drowning her last shred of hope with its golden appeal.

Desperation exploded inside Rachel. She glanced at Josh to see that he was still occupied with his coloring, then she strode straight up to the bar, anger and frustration building almost as fast as the fear. She glared at Sloan's unyielding profile and summoned the courage to defy his dismissal.

"I know what he did to you," Rachel told him, her voice quaking with emotion she could no more hide than she could stop breathing. "I know about your wife and son."

He stilled, the drink almost to his lips. A muscle flexed in his rigid jaw and his knuckles whitened around the glass. Slowly, with exacting precision, Sloan placed the untouched liquor back on the counter. He turned and stared at her, the full impact of his size slamming into Rachel for the first time. He was tall, with massive shoulders. He was more man than she had ever been this close to before. A new kind of tension zipped through her, adding to her already unbearable apprehension.

"Since you seem to know so much about my experience with Angel," Sloan suggested with equal measures sarcasm and contempt, "why don't you tell me what fascination you hold for the son of a bitch."

Rachel's throat constricted. She swallowed, but it didn't help. "He wants my son."

Sloan glanced at Josh. Josh was busy selecting another crayon from the well-worn box. Rachel's heart threatened to burst from her chest. Would this man help her when she told him the rest? *Please God,* she prayed, *please don't let him turn us away.* Not now. They had come so far.

Distrust or maybe disbelief flickered in Sloan's otherwise emotionless eyes. ''Why would he want your son?''

Everything inside Rachel stilled as she stared into the eyes of the only man on earth who could help her. And what she was about to tell him would likely be the very reason he would not.

''Because Josh is Angel's son, too.''

IT TOOK A FULL ten seconds for the words Rachel Larson uttered to fully assimilate in Sloan's brain. His gaze shifted to the dark-haired boy seated a couple of tables away. As if feeling Sloan's gaze on him, the boy looked up. Wide, curious eyes stared back at Sloan. The same black eyes that haunted Sloan whenever he tried to sleep without getting half wasted first. A tremor started someplace deep inside him, like an earthquake before it reaches the surface of the earth. Sloan's right hand shook and he curled his fingers into a tight fist. Something dark and ugly filtered through Sloan's mind, but he pushed it away.

This was Angel's son. Sloan didn't need to see a birth certificate; the proof was written all over the boy's face. He was a mirror image of his father. Sloan averted his gaze and blinked to dispel the image that somehow evolved into a full-grown version of Angel. Sloan reminded himself that this was only a child, innocent of his father's heinous crimes.

"What do you want?" Sloan heard himself say, his voice so cold and hard that he barely recognized it as his own.

"I need your help," she repeated, her tone low and pleading.

Sloan blew out a breath. "Yeah, well, you said that already." He leveled his gaze on huge brown eyes that made his gut clench with an old feeling that was familiar yet alien to the man he had become. He squashed the protective instincts that rose automatically at the sight of this needy young woman and her son.... Angel's son.

Sloan swallowed. Hard.

"Exactly what kind of help is it that you think you need from me, Miss…"

"Rachel Larson," she told him again.

Sloan studied the woman as she worked up the nerve to spell out what she wanted from him. She was a real looker if a guy liked his woman a little on the skinny side. From the dark circles under her eyes though, Sloan would lay odds that she didn't sleep long or often. But all that thick brown hair hanging around her shoulders was her saving grace…and the lips. She had those full, kissable lips that any man breathing would lust after. The blouse and long flowing skirt were too loose and concealing to determine if there were any curves at all hidden beneath them. Strappy sandals with sensible heels adorned her feet. It wasn't until his gaze collided with hers again that Sloan realized she hadn't spoken yet because she was too busy fighting the urge to turn tail and run. His blatant appraisal had seriously disturbed her shaky bravado.

"No matter where we go," she finally burst out, then caught herself. She took a calming breath. A combination of frustration and fear danced across her pretty face. "Or how many times we move, he always finds us." She clasped the shoulder strap of her bag more tightly. "The last time he found us he told me that he was tired of my running and that very soon he was going to take Josh…and…and then he would have no further use for me." She blinked furiously to hold back the tears threatening. "I don't know what else to do. You're our only hope."

Sloan mentally stepped back from what every instinct urged him to feel. He refused to feel any of this. It was a hell of a sad story but it had nothing to do with him. Angel's former lovers held no interest for Sloan. Besides, this sounded too good to be true. That someone Angel might care about, with his son in tow, would waltz into Los Laureles looking for Sloan's help seemed a bit too pat. This had setup written all over it. Still, she had said that Victoria sent her.

"Sounds like a domestic problem to me, Miss Larson," he suggested, testing the waters of sincerity. Sloan pressed her with a steely glare intended to intimidate. "And I'm no social worker." She faltered, but didn't scurry away as he fully expected.

"I don't need a social worker," she said with determination, and a hefty dose of bitterness. "I need someone who can protect my son from Angel."

Still skeptical, Sloan cocked his head and eyed her speculatively. "Call a cop," he offered.

The flash of anger that brightened her eyes took Sloan by surprise. He almost smiled, but he was too busy watching the metamorphosis in Rachel Larson.

"You know the police can't help me," she returned with barely controlled fury.

"Then tell me, Miss Larson," he goaded. "What is it you think I can do that the police can't."

The look that passed between them proved immensely more telling than the words that followed. "Angel will come for his son. I want you to do whatever it takes to stop him."

A long silence followed, but her fiery gaze never wavered. She was dead serious, Sloan realized then. Rachel Larson wanted him to do the one thing he had longed to have the opportunity to do for seven endless years. She wanted him to kill Gabriel DiCassi.

Time had not dulled his fierce desire for vengeance, only the urgency of it. His wife and son were dead. Nothing could change that. Sloan set his jaw hard against the paralyzing emotions that wanted to surface even now, after all this time. The finality had crashed down around him long ago, after almost a year of nonstop searching for Angel. Grief and the need to avenge his wife and son had kept him looking when everyone else had given up. The realization that nothing he did would matter, it sure as hell wouldn't bring them back, hit him eventually. Then there was nothing. He stopped feeling anything at all.

But now anticipation surged anew through Sloan's veins. The mere notion of killing Angel made him almost giddy. His gaze traveled back to the boy. The woman was even providing the perfect bait. How far would a piece of crap like Angel be willing to go for his own son? A strange calm settled over Sloan then. He knew just how far any man would go. And he wouldn't have to do anything but wait Angel out. Long buried sensations bombarded Sloan. A dozen snippets of memory flashed through his mind. He closed his eyes in overwhelming despair when the sound of his son's cries echoed through his soul. Sloan wanted to kill Angel more than he wanted to draw in his next breath. For the first time, Sloan had the perfect means by which to lure him.

Sloan opened his eyes to the woman standing before him. Self-disgust abruptly made him sick to his stomach. Uncharacteristic moisture stung his eyes. Had he fallen so very far? He shook his head. What kind of man would use a woman and child to assuage his own savage thirst for revenge? Sloan swallowed the answer that welled in his throat, the answer he didn't want to acknowledge. But it was there, it had always been there. The urge was so strong that Sloan could taste it. Not one doubt had ever existed in his mind that, if given the opportunity, he would do anything, give anything, within his power to make Angel pay for what he had done.

But not this.

He would not use a child. He could not. Not even Angel's child.

He leveled his gaze on Rachel's and with his next words affirmed his decision, "I'm not the man you need for the job."

Sloan walked away without looking back.

He pushed through the swinging doors and into the harsh light of day. He lifted his face to the sun's warm kiss and drew in a ragged breath. No point wasting any effort on regret. There would be a day of reckoning, he had no doubt. He would take Angel down, Sloan had made that vow long ago. But he would never stoop to Angel's level to do it. Sloan could not—would not—use a child.

Cool, soft fingers touched Sloan's arm. He pivoted

and glowered down at the woman who had followed him from the cantina.

"I told you I'm not the man for the job," he growled. The little boy cowered behind his mother now, cautiously peeking past her skirt. Sloan swore under his breath. Now he was scaring small children.

Rachel held her ground, meeting his lethal glare with lead in her own. "You're the only man for the job," she insisted with quiet strength.

"Lady, you've got a hell of a lot of nerve coming to a place like this." He gestured at all that surrounded them. "Do you have a clue the kind of men you walked past in there?" He stepped closer to her, putting himself in her personal space now and forcing her to acknowledge his superior physical strength. "Florescitaf is the bottom of the barrel down here. There are sleazebags here that would sell their own mother for their next drink. Any one of them could eat you alive and not blink. I'm surprised you made it this far."

She opened her mouth to speak, then hesitated. "I had to come here," she said finally. "This is where you are. And I need you."

Sloan shook his head. Victoria had no business sending this woman and her son to him. He wasn't a do-gooder anymore. Sloan took the jobs no one else wanted to take. The ones too dangerous for a man who cared whether he lived or died.

"I'm no knight in shining armor, Miss Larson. In fact, I'm so far from it that most women who know my reputation wouldn't consider themselves safe this close." He allowed his gaze to rove the length of her once more for good measure. "You're sure it's me you're looking for?"

Uncertain now, she shifted nervously. "Victoria said

you're the best. She said you know Angel." She licked her full lips. To Sloan's irritation, he followed the movement with growing interest. "She said," Rachel continued, "that if there was anyone who could help me, it was you."

"Like I told you before, Victoria made a mistake." He started to turn away, but something in those big, pleading eyes stayed him.

"You know what he'll do," she murmured. Tears slipped past those long lashes and streamed down her cheeks. "Can you turn your back on us knowing what he'll do?"

Sloan looked away. He didn't want to see or hear any of this. He wanted to go back into the cantina and finish off that bottle he left on the bar. He wanted to forget the name Gabriel DiCassi. He wanted to erase the image of this woman and her son from his mind. But he could never do either of those things.

"Josh!"

Sloan jerked his attention back to Rachel. She whirled around, calling her son's name. Josh was nowhere in sight.

"Oh God, where can he be?" Rachel rushed forward, then hesitated as if unsure which way to go. "He was right behind me.... Josh!"

Sloan's heart pumped hard in his chest. The vivid memory of endless days and nights of searching for his own son broadsided him with the force of a runaway train. The first moment of realization that his little boy was not at home...not at the neighbor's...not anywhere. A cold sweat coated Sloan's skin. The final gut-wrenching instant when he had to admit defeat. His son was dead...murdered. Sloan shuddered, then trembled with remembered pain so sharp that nausea burned the back of his throat.

"Josh!" Rachel cried out, her voice riddled with hysteria and the panic no doubt tightening like a steel band around her chest. She zigzagged in and out of the throngs of people milling from shop to shop.

Siesta had long passed and the streets were filled with shoppers and peddlers going about their business as the heat of the day slowly subsided with the retreating sun. Children played in the alleys and the streets. Dogs barked and sniffed about, looking for handouts. The occasional car horn honked to clear the way as it inched past on the cluttered cobblestone street.

Sloan scanned face after face, each distracted with his or her own agenda. Another handful of children skipped past, chattering and laughing. But none proved to be the one he was searching for.

Josh was gone.

Sloan moved toward Rachel, then caught her by the elbow and pulled her around to face him. He pinned her with a steady gaze, hoping to calm the fear dancing in hers. "Stay right here, out in the open where Josh can see you." Another tear streaked downward. Before he could stop himself Sloan reached up and swiped that tear from her soft check with the pad of his thumb. "I will find him," he promised, then turned away.

Josh couldn't have gone far on his own....

Chapter Two

Rachel's frantic search stalled in the middle of the street. Sloan's warning to stay where Josh could see her belatedly echoed in her ears. She watched in utter despair as Sloan came out of the last shop empty-handed. Her heart pounded so hard that her chest ached with each heavy thud. She wanted to run through the streets screaming her agony, but her arms and legs felt like useless wooden clubs. This couldn't be happening. The nightmare she feared most had reached long bony fingers from the blackest depths of her subconscious and climbed into her reality.

Josh was gone.

They had looked everywhere.

Sloan paused near a group of children and spoke to them in fluent Spanish. All other sound except his voice faded into insignificance. The children shook their heads in a sort of surreal harmony. No, they had not seen an American boy. Rachel blinked, once, twice. This was her fault. She had taken her eyes off Josh for just one moment and—

A horn blasted behind her. Strong hands jerked her forward and against a hard wall of muscle.

"Dammit, woman, you're going to get yourself

killed,'' Sloan growled, the sound rumbling from his massive chest.

Beyond caring whose strong arms were around her, Rachel wilted against him. The tears she could no longer restrain flowed from her, bleeding out the last of her resolve in salty rivulets. She fisted her fingers into the soft cotton of Sloan's faded shirt and fought to hold on to consciousness. She could not give in to the relief her exhausted body propelled her toward. She had to find Josh. She couldn't live without her son. She had to find him…to protect him.

With renewed determination Rachel pushed away from Sloan, oddly bereft without his powerful arms around her now. But she had to do something. She couldn't just stand here. She swiped the moisture from her cheeks and stared up into those piercing blue eyes. "He has to be here…"

"I told you I would find him and I will. But I can't look for him and keep you out of trouble at the same time." The irritation in his voice manifested itself in a line between his eyebrows.

The look of concern that emanated from Sloan's gaze frightened Rachel all the more. If a man like Sloan was worried, then the situation must look pretty hopeless. A tremor shook her. No. She wouldn't believe that. Josh couldn't have gone far. He was just curious that's all. Sloan was right. He was probably exploring and had wandered out of sight. The goats had captured his attention earlier. And the children…

"I have to look for him, too." Dragging in an uneven breath, Rachel averted her gaze from the one watching her so very intently. She dug furiously through her bag until she found a recent snapshot of her son. Armed with the only weapon she possessed, her determination, she hurried to catch up with the children who were slowly meandering down the street. With both of them looking they could cover more ground.

"Excuse me." Rachel displayed Josh's picture. Maybe they would remember seeing him if they knew what he looked like. A half-dozen sets of dark expectant eyes looked first at Rachel then at the picture she held in her trembling hand. "My son...my *niño* is lost." Rachel moistened her lips and forced herself to take a breath. The blood roared in her ears. She wanted to cry again. Her mind whirled, making concentration difficult, but she had to focus on finding Josh. The children only looked at each other, then at her and shook their heads. Frustration twisted inside Rachel. Surely someone had seen him.

He couldn't have simply disappeared into thin air.

Unless...Angel was here already. Overwhelming dread pooled in Rachel's stomach. No...he couldn't have known she was coming here. He couldn't have found her so quickly.

Rachel felt strangely detached from her surroundings. She squeezed her eyes shut to chase away the black spots and to slow the spinning in her head.

"Mommy!"

Sloan was the first to spot the boy. Josh stood on the other side of the street. To Sloan it looked as if someone had just left him there. Instinct pricked him. This didn't feel right. Sloan waited for a rusty old truck to chug past then he ran to the boy. He crouched in front of him and surveyed him for injury. Profound relief raced through Sloan's veins, chasing away the suspicions niggling at him. The kid was fine.

Josh's lips protruded into a pout. "I want my mommy," he muttered, tears welling in his dark eyes.

Rachel was suddenly on her knees next to Sloan. She hugged her son so close Sloan was sure the kid couldn't possibly be breathing. Rachel was crying and kissing Josh and telling him how much she loved him.

Sloan stood and looked away.

What the hell was he doing with this woman and her child? They aren't your problem, he told himself firmly. It wasn't his fault that Rachel Larson had herself in a no-win situation. Sloan would just send them back to Victoria on the next flight out of Chihuahua. The last thing he needed or wanted was complications. And this lady and her kid were definitely complicated. They reminded him too much of the past...of what he had lost. And even if Angel did care enough about his kid to come for him, Sloan had no desire to start a war with a woman and child caught in the middle.

No way.

"Josh," Rachel said hesitantly. "Where did you get this bear?"

Sloan's gaze swung back to the boy. Rachel pulled Josh's hand from behind his back. He quickly hugged what appeared to be a small brown bear to his chest.

"It's s'posed t'be a secret, Mommy," the boy whispered too loudly. His doubtful gaze darted up to Sloan, then widened with distrust.

"Look at me, Josh." Rachel held him firmly by both shoulders. "Where did you get the bear?"

Josh huffed a big breath. "It's a present from my daddy." He turned the bear to his mother then so that she could see his prize. "See."

Recognition slammed into Sloan. The bear with its big button eyes and red ribbon tied neatly around the neck mocked him. Sloan's son had cherished a bear very much like this one. The bear had been found with his...*body*. Sloan had buried the toy with his child. Sloan tugged the bear from Josh's grasp and inspected it more closely.

Josh wailed his protests. Rachel pulled him to her and tried to quiet him, her face stricken with a mixture of fear and desperation. She was thinking the same thing Sloan was. He could see it in her eyes.

As if in slow motion, Sloan turned all the way around, his gaze searching every face, every shop window, every shadow.

Could Angel be this close?

Anticipation ignited the adrenaline already flowing with the wild hammering in his chest. His attention still tracking every move around them, Sloan passed the bear back to Rachel.

"Let's go."

Rachel stood, Josh clutched tightly in her arms. "What do you mean?" Hope flashed in her eyes.

Sloan shot her a look that quelled any other questions she might have asked, "You're coming with me." A new kind of evil just rolled into town, he didn't add.

RACHEL FELT COMPLETELY drained. She glanced over the seat at Josh who was preoccupied with his new bear. Fear twisted inside her each time she recalled Josh's words. *It's a present from my daddy.* The more distance they put between them and the town the calmer Rachel felt.

Once Sloan had ushered them into his Jeep the interrogation had begun. Sloan wanted to know every detail of every moment Josh had been out of their sight.

It didn't seem to matter to Sloan that a four-year-old had no concept of time. Josh explained that he had followed one of the children who was chasing a dog and had gotten lost. When he couldn't find his mommy he simply sat down and cried. A nice dark-haired lady, according to Josh, had come along and told him not to cry and that she had a gift for him from his daddy. Then she had led Josh to where he could find his mommy.

The lady's description matched most every woman in this country, including Rachel's. She consoled herself with the belief that perhaps some kind lady had offered comfort to a lost child and then helped him find his way back to his mother. Maybe the woman hadn't had time for pleasantries, or didn't care about being thanked.

Sloan was far more skeptical of Josh's story. He had his own theory, though he hadn't felt compelled to share his thoughts as of yet. But Rachel knew he was convinced Angel had something to do with it. Whatever motivated him, Rachel was grateful that he had changed his mind and decided to help them. The concern he had shown when she couldn't find Josh warmed her, and gave her hope that Sloan wasn't really as bad as he pretended to be.

But then, Rachel was a die-hard optimist.

She stared out at the passing landscape. The desert seemed to swallow them up almost as soon as they left Florescitaf. The sun was dropping even lower now, casting purple and pink hues like a halo around the descending ball of fire. And with it went the oppressive heat. Rachel shivered and chafed her bare arms with her hands to warm them against the cooler wind whipping through the open Jeep now.

"There's a jacket in the back seat if you're cold."

Rachel glanced at Sloan's unyielding profile. He could have been carved right out of the rugged Sierra Madre mountains that jutted skyward before them. How odd that he would show concern for her comfort when he had scarcely spoken a word since they left town except to question Josh. She couldn't decide which persona she liked best. The Sloan who defined indifference, or the fleeting moments of the other man who obviously lay beneath all that bitterness and attitude. He hadn't even named his price for the services he apparently intended to render. Now that Rachel thought about it, the fact of the matter was she had no idea where they were headed. His home, she assumed. A rustic cabin or a tent were the first images to pop into her mind. Sloan didn't appear the type to put much stock in personal possessions.

"Thanks, but I'm fine," she said, in response to his offer of the jacket. Rachel focused her attention on the dusty road in front of them and asked, "Where are we going?"

"My place." The answer was curt, and spoken grudgingly.

Iceman was back. Instinct told her that Sloan didn't want anyone close to him. It would behoove her to keep her distance. His momentary lapse of concern had obviously passed.

"Our things are at the hotel," Rachel realized aloud, only now remembering that they had checked into a hotel when they arrived the day before. With no idea how long it would take her to find Sloan or to persuade him to take her case, it had seemed like the right thing to do. But with Josh getting lost, sensible thinking had gone out the window.

"I'll take care of it tomorrow."

"Thank you." He said nothing. Determined to ignore his lack of social grace and to listen to her own instincts, Rachel leaned back into her seat and tried to relax. After two days without sleep, she was spent physically. She had no idea when she had eaten last either. In all honesty, food no longer held any appeal for her. Eating equated to survival. She survived for one reason and one reason only, to protect her son. Nothing else mattered at this point.

Sloan slowed and took a left, heading directly into the more rugged terrain that led to the foothills of the Sierra Madre. The Jeep bumped over the rough road for another mile or so before Sloan slowed once more. The mountains loomed in the distance, their jagged peaks rising to the clouds to greet the darkening sky. The landscape that lay ahead sharply contrasted the sprawling desert land they had covered so far. Desert scrub and cacti eventually gave way to trees that sprouted up from the towering mountainous terrain.

Rachel saw the wall first, then the roof of the house that lay beyond it. She bent forward slightly, and stifled a gasp. The place looked like a modern-day fortress. A towering wall, at least ten or twelve feet high, surrounded the house. A huge iron gate stood before them when Sloan stopped the Jeep. He pressed a series of buttons on a keypad by the gate. The massive iron gates opened immediately, then closed automatically behind them. Rachel watched in a sort of surprised bewilderment as they drove away from the intimidating entrance.

Sloan parked before the double doors at the front of the southwestern-style house. The exterior was a stucco finish, painted a pinkish tan like the wall surrounding

the property. The roof was a rustic red tile. One of the
front doors suddenly opened and a short, thin man
stepped out to meet them.

"This is where you live?" Rachel asked, then
winced. God, what a stupid question. Of course this
was where he lived.

"Ever since I ran off the local drug lord," he said
before hopping out of the Jeep.

Rachel frowned. Was that supposed to be a joke?
Did she really want to know? Too tired to consider the
remark any further, Rachel unfastened her seat belt and
leaned between the bucket seats and released Josh's.
The boy, teddy bear in tow, scrambled out of the seat
and into his mother's arms. Rachel settled Josh onto
the ground once they were out of the Jeep. Sloan was
speaking to the other man in Spanish. Rachel couldn't
quite get the gist of the conversation. Something about
a room, and trouble.

She and Josh were the trouble, of course.

"Good evening, Señora Larson," the man said, his
smile wide and pleasant. "I am Pablo. I am very sure
that you are hungry. Come in and I will prepare a
proper feast for such honored guests."

Rachel took an instant liking to the man. She returned Pablo's smile and followed as he led the way
into the house. Rachel could feel Sloan behind her. She
didn't have to look, his formidable presence was unmistakable. There was an aura about the man that en-
tailed much more than his air of danger.

Details flooded her senses. Muted colors, thick up-
holstered furnishings. Rachel had to admit that she had
been way off base about the man's taste in accom-
modations. Sloan's home was elegant in an understated
sort of way. Her artist's eye was drawn to the clean

lines and sparse but inviting furnishings of each large room she passed. The expansive hall cut through the middle of the house, flowing both left and right about midway. Pablo turned right and continued until they reached the third room on the left.

He gestured for Rachel to enter before him. "If there is anything you need, *señora,* do not hesitate to ask."

"Thank you, Pablo," she said tiredly.

"I'm hungry!" Josh piped up.

Heat scalded Rachel's cheeks. Josh was always hungry. "Josh," she scolded.

"The boy needs to eat," Pablo agreed. "Come with Pablo, little man, and we will prepare the feast together." Pablo winked when Josh eyed him hesitantly. "You may taste as we go."

Josh was ready to go then. He took Pablo's offered hand and told him about his new bear as they disappeared down the hall. Rachel was amazed at how easily Josh befriended the strangers he met. She thought of the woman and the bear and decided that a long talk with her son was in order.

With Josh and Pablo gone, Rachel had no choice but to acknowledge her host's brooding presence. She turned hesitantly to face him.

"I don't know why you changed your mind," Rachel began, trying hard not to allow that icy blue gaze to undo her. "But I—"

"You should eat and get some rest," he said, his words an order rather than a suggestion.

He turned to go but Rachel stopped him with a hand on his arm. He stared first at her hand then at her, as if her touch were somehow offensive to him. But the feel of his skin beneath her fingertips was anything but offensive to Rachel. She jerked her hand back when a mild shock radiated through her, but caught herself before she frowned.

"I'd like to discuss your plans," she managed in a surprisingly even voice. "I don't want to be left in the dark. I need to know what you have in mind."

For one long moment his gaze held hers and something intense passed between them. For Rachel, it felt all too much like sexual awareness. Sloan was handsome, in a fierce, rugged way. He was big and muscular and with eyes that could unsettle her with just a look. He frightened her, yet drew her on some level that Rachel could never hope to explain. Maybe it was simply the need to feel protected by someone who was strong enough to go up against Angel.

"I don't have a plan." His gaze remained unreadable, as seemed customary for him. "I'll let you know when we have anything to discuss." He brushed past Rachel and sauntered in the direction into which Josh and Pablo had disappeared.

Rachel leaned against the door frame, crossed her arms over her chest and sighed wearily. The man's attitude infuriated her. How on earth would she ever tolerate his rude indifference? Rachel was too tired to contemplate the issue any further at the moment. She was so tired she wasn't even sure she would make it through dinner. For Josh's sake she would have to muster up the energy to at least show up, then see to her son's bath and to get him tucked into bed. And just maybe, she could manage a leisurely bath of her own.

She glanced around the spacious room she and Josh were to share. She thought of the property's elaborate security system, and then of Sloan himself. Despite her enigmatic protector's personality, or lack thereof, Rachel felt safe for the first time in nearly five years.

SLOAN STARED AT the bottle of tequila on the table before him. He knew there would be no sleep for him tonight, no matter how much he drank. His mind was reeling with bits of information he didn't want to remember. Faces he didn't want to see. Voices he didn't want to hear. But there were certain points he had to allow himself to recall. He had waited too long, planned too often for this very moment, yet feared it would never come. Not once since pulling himself from the gutter pain and depression had hurled him into had he allowed a glimmer of real hope. Anticipation was one thing, but hope entirely another. He'd learned the hard way that hope was only for those too weak to acknowledge defeat when it had them by the throat.

Sloan had faced defeat, but he hadn't wallowed in it, at least not for long. He couldn't change history, but he sure as hell had some say in the future. And he would make Angel pay. Very soon.

To Sloan's supreme irritation the vivid mental image of Rachel Larson suddenly loomed large in his mind. He could still hear the fear and panic in her voice when she called out for Josh. That same desperation had haunted his own voice seven years ago. The euphoria still lingered from the profound relief he had felt this evening when Josh was in his mother's arms once more. The relief he had been denied seven years ago. Then the realization that Angel might be close by.

Too close.

Sloan shook off the feelings nagging him, but he couldn't completely shake the picture of Rachel. The fear in those big brown eyes, the way her lips quivered with uncertainty. If anyone he had met in this business had ever needed protecting, she sure as hell did. But Sloan wanted to do more than protect her, he wanted

to know her as a woman. That simple touch this eve-
ning in her room had sent fire raging through his veins.
For the first time in more years than he cared to admit,
Sloan yearned for more than mere physical release.

Ire burned in his gut. He couldn't feel this way.

It was nothing more than his exaggerated instinct to
protect. That's all, he assured himself.

Angel flickered amid the other tangle of images and
thoughts involving Rachel Larson. Sloan swore. His
attraction to a woman who had once been involved
with Angel made Sloan's gut clench. Those feelings
were a betrayal to the memory of his wife and son. He
must be losing his mind to entertain such a fantasy.
Hell, he had already lost his mind. He had brought
Angel's son into his own home.

Sloan swore repeatedly.

He hated himself for what he was doing. But it was
the ultimate goal that made it all worthwhile. Angel
would come for his son. It was the basic concept of
possession. The kid belonged to him. Angel would
want him back, so he had to come. When he did, Sloan
would be ready.

And Angel would die.

Then Rachel and Josh would be safe.

That wasn't supposed to be what counted to
Sloan...but somehow it was. Somehow their welfare
already meant entirely too much to him. And that
didn't sit well with him. But he would not let either of
them any closer. He would stay in control—no matter
what it took. All these jumbled feelings were nothing
more than his deeply entrenched need to protect those
weaker than him.

The way he couldn't protect his own wife and son.

"Excuse me."

Sloan's head shot up at the softly uttered greeting. Rachel Larson hovered near the door. Hesitantly she stepped out onto the patio and approached him, her bare feet soundless on the cool tile. His gaze followed her movements, his body automatically responding and he silently cursed himself again. He was a fool. Sloan leaned back in his chair and leveled an impatient gaze in her direction.

"I prefer drinking alone, Miss Larson," Sloan said tersely. "So if you're looking for company, you'll find Pablo's more to your liking."

Rachel hesitated a few feet away from the table. "I...I just wanted to thank you for helping us. I realized after I put Josh to bed that I hadn't properly thanked you for allowing us refuge in your home."

Sloan tossed back the tequila in his shot glass and set the empty glass down next to the bottle. The last thing he needed was her gratitude distorting the already fuzzy scenario taking shape in his head. "Don't thank me, *Miss Larson,* I'm not doing it for you." He poured himself another shot. "I'm doing it for me."

Rachel nodded mutely. "Of course," she murmured. "Well, good night then."

Before she could turn away, and to Sloan's royal irritation, he stopped her. "There is one thing you can do for me," he said, his words dripping contempt, his senses already piqued in anticipation of her response. "You can tell me how you managed to get yourself *intimately* involved with a lowlife scum bag like Angel."

Rachel visibly faltered. She seemed to struggle with her answer for so long that Sloan felt certain she didn't plan to tell him. She shoved a handful of that thick dark hair behind her ear and drew in a deep breath.

When her gaze finally connected with his again, her eyes were suspiciously bright. His gut clenched. Sloan swore another silent oath.

"I was very young, just nineteen," she began slowly. "He tricked me into believing he was someone he wasn't." She swallowed, the effort required displayed along the delicate column of her pale throat. "My father died because of what I allowed to happen. If I hadn't..." She fell silent, her eyes downcast.

Sloan's chair scraped across the tile as he pushed back from the table and stood. Her head snapped up and she shivered as he walked deliberately toward her. When he stopped, he stood only inches from her. She tensed, and her breath caught with a little hitch. Damn him, he wanted to touch her. Anger swirled around him, inside him. He didn't need this.

"You allowed yourself to be seduced by the bastard while he was plotting to kill your own father?" Sloan hurled the words at her like missiles intended to wound, intended to push her away. Hadn't he done the same damned thing? Seduced by the challenge of the hunt, he had dogged Angel's every step until the animal retaliated. Years of pent-up rage unleashed inside Sloan at the thought.

He leaned closer to Rachel, directing that unforgiving energy at her, widening the emotional gap between them. "I guess that makes us both pretty stupid, huh? Neither one of us were smart enough to know what we were up against until it was too late."

She trembled, but held her ground. "He tricked me. I didn't know—"

"Yeah, well that was a tough break for your old man, wasn't it?"

Her anger flared finally, however faintly. "I don't

want to discuss this any more.'' She pivoted and started toward the door.

Sloan snagged her by the arm and swung her around to face him. He ignored the electricity that crackled where his hand closed around her bare skin. ''You screwed up, just like I did.'' He pulled her closer, his body's response to hers only fueling his building anger. She glared up at him, her own anger taking belated shape. ''You've come all this way looking for a miracle. And what do you know? I'm fresh out. Maybe you'd better rethink your strategy.''

''You're our only hope.'' Her sweet, desperate breath fanned his lips.

Sloan clenched his teeth and shook his head, every muscle in his body growing harder by the moment. ''Maybe you think coming here is the answer to your prayers, but you're wrong. I'm just a man, Rachel Larson. I'll take Angel down, but that won't change what he took from you or me. I'm no superhero, and I'm sure as hell no saint. But if you hang around long enough the one thing I can guarantee you is that you'll end up in my bed.''

Sloan saw it coming, but he didn't try to stop her. Her right palm connected with his jaw. He took the blow, because he deserved it. The pain was somehow cleansing. Pain he could handle, these other feelings he couldn't.

Rachel jerked weakly at his fierce hold on her left arm. ''Let me go.''

''You went to a lot of trouble to track me down,'' he rasped as he snaked his arm around her waist and hauled her up against him. ''Don't you want to find out if I'm half the man you seem to think I am?''

The dam broke loose then, tears trickled down her

face. She pushed uselessly against his chest. "I already know all I need to know." She was shaking uncontrollably now. "I saw how you reacted when you thought Josh was lost. You're a good man. I know you are."

Sloan had no come back for that allegation. He could only stare into those deep brown eyes, watery with the kind of pain he understood all too well. Just when he felt certain that he would have to kiss her...kiss her or die, she wilted in his fierce hold. Startled, Sloan scooped her slight body into his arms.

Damn.

She had been through too much. He had pushed her too hard. All because he couldn't control his own sadistic impulses.

Sloan considered the sweet, innocent-looking woman lying unconscious in his arms for a long moment. He shook his head in self-disgust.

"I told you I was no knight in shining armor." He let go a mighty breath. "What am I supposed to do with you now?"

Chapter Three

Rachel moaned contentedly and snuggled into her pillow. Her lids slowly opened to the realization that it was now daylight. The last vestiges of sleep retreated bringing awareness one degree at a time. The fluffy pillow beneath her cheek, the cool sheet over her body, and the slight breeze whispering across her face. She inhaled deeply of a scent that was at once alien and soothing. A pleasant masculine scent, musk and leather.

Sloan.

Rachel's eyes opened wide. She surveyed the part of the room readily viewable without having to move. This was not the same room Pablo had shown her and Josh to last evening. Her heart pounded in her chest as last night's heated words with Sloan replayed in her head. She remembered collapsing…

Her attention suddenly lit on the puddle of clothing a few feet away on the carpeted floor. Her blouse, her skirt and sandals. The fact that being on the small side in the bust allowed her to go braless most of the time slammed into her. She sat bolt upright on the side of the bed and looked down at herself. She wore what appeared to be a man's T-shirt. Too large for Pablo's.

She swallowed tightly. Sloan's. She looked around the room and realization dawned with unnerving clarity.

She was in Sloan's room. In his bed.

Rachel spun around to look on the other side of the bed. It was empty.

Where was Josh?

Fear rushed through her limbs to lodge in her chest. She had tucked him into bed in the other room. She blinked, forcing herself to concentrate rather than losing herself to the panic. Maybe he was having breakfast already. What time was it? Her gaze sought out the nearest clock. The LED display on the bedside table read 10:00 a.m. Rachel shot to her feet. How could she have slept so long?

Where was her son?

Laughter floated through the open window. *Josh.* Rachel bounded off the bed and to the generous windows. She peered out into the backyard. Sheer, gauzy drapes fluttered around her in the gentle breeze. With Pablo watching, Josh chased a bright red ball. His delighted squeals and laughter brought the first relaxed smile to her lips in too long to remember. It felt so good to see her son play without worry that someone would snatch him away from her. Pablo tossed the ball again, and Josh's enthusiastic race for the brightly colored, bouncing object gladdened her heart. This was all she had ever wanted for her son…for him to feel happy and safe.

Taking stock of the area for the first time in daylight, Rachel amended her earlier impression. This was not a backyard, this was a courtyard. As beautiful as any she had ever seen. And she had seen a few while growing up. Rachel's smile faded as she considered the bittersweet memories of growing up with her father. Her mother had died when she was only a small child. But her father had made up for the loss many times over. He took Rachel everywhere with him. A well-respected figure in the State Department, they had traveled frequently, abroad mostly. The hotels were always luxurious. But she had yet to view a courtyard any more spectacular than Sloan's.

Elegant tile or cobblestone pavers covered what was most likely a sandy yard. The house surrounded the courtyard on all sides, adding to the feeling of security. Numerous sets of French doors opened onto the courtyard from the rooms facing it, including the one in which she now stood. Lush foliage, mostly tropical, probably native to the area, nearly camouflaged a sparkling pool. Beyond the house, a water tank towered, supplying the residence with water despite the sprawling desert that surrounded it. The word fortress flitted through Rachel's mind again. She wondered if there were generators and a bountiful food supply stored somewhere on the grounds, making the place self-sufficient despite the desolation and its remoteness.

Relieved that Josh was safe, Rachel pushed her other curiosities from her mind. She would ask Sloan more questions when the opportunity presented itself. For now, she should get dressed and join her son outside. She had a feeling that Sloan would let her know what he wanted from her, monetarily and otherwise, when he made up his mind or developed some plan. He didn't strike her as the sort of man one could hurry.

Finding her reluctant host watching from the open doorway, Rachel gasped. That unreadable blue gaze traveled down the length of her, then back to connect with hers. Her state of undress sent a flush of heat up her neck and across her cheeks. She edged closer to the sheer material hanging around her for some sense of protection from his all-seeing gaze.

The sound that rumbled from his chest was more growl than laugh. "Don't be shy, Miss Larson, I've already seen all there is to see."

He had undressed her last night, then again just now with his eyes. On some level she had already known that Sloan was the one. Though she preferred to undress herself, Pablo having done so would have been a great deal less humiliating alternative. To her chagrin, her nipples tightened at the thought that Sloan had looked at her so intimately. That was not an appropriate reaction, she reminded herself with rising indignation.

"I'd like to get dressed now," she announced, hoping he would take the hint and leave.

"Your suitcase is in your room. Pablo picked it up this morning, along with a few other things I told him you would need." A holster, complete with sleek black gun, was strapped to one broad shoulder. He crossed his arms over his mile-wide chest and leaned against the door frame.

Rachel tried not to follow the distracting movement of powerful muscle. She moistened her lips and asked the question that tightened the back of her throat. "Why did you bring me to your...in here?" Surely she would remember if anything happened. She couldn't have been that far out of it. She shivered at the thought of those strong hands touching her bare skin.

"The boy was asleep. I didn't want to wake him."

Somehow she sensed that there was more to it than that. He hadn't wanted to be in the same room with Josh—even for a few minutes, she suddenly realized. "I don't usually...react like that," she began in explanation of what he probably considered weakness. She squared her shoulders and stepped away from the meager protection the drapes provided. Somehow she had to learn to hold her own in the man's presence. "Despite how it may look to you now, I am a strong person."

He straightened. Rachel jumped, instantly making a liar out of herself. Sloan crossed the room to stand directly in front of her. He stared down at her for a long moment before he spoke. Rachel had the distinct impression he was trying to read her mind. The same scent that lingered on the crisp white sheets of his bed emanated from his big, powerful body. The T-shirt he wore molded to his chest, outlining every ripple and contour. The sweatpants concealed little of his masculine assets.

"Strong willed, yes," he finally said. "That's probably what has kept you alive until now." His gaze slid slowly over her body once more. Rachel shivered. "But," he continued, "physically you're weak. That makes all that willpower useless in the end."

She knew without analyzing his words that she had just been insulted. But Rachel also knew full well that he was right. "That's why I came to you. You have the strength and the know how to protect us."

"When Angel comes—" Sloan glanced out the window, his gaze tracking Josh's energetic romp, then quickly moving to something else "—it won't be for me." His gaze returned to Rachel's. "He'll come for you and the boy. You have to be prepared to protect yourself."

Rachel swallowed at the lump of uncertainty clogging her throat. "Isn't that the service you're supposed to provide?"

He made a sound of distaste in his throat. "Lady,

I'm not about to get myself killed trying to help someone who isn't willing to help herself.''

Irritation grated her nerves. "I do the best I can. Fighting and eluding madmen weren't choices on the curriculum in any of the schools I attended."

Anger flickered in his steely gaze then. "Well, maybe it should have been, and just maybe you wouldn't be in this predicament now."

"What's that supposed to mean?"

"It means," he growled, his expression fierce, "that there's no time like the present to get your act together." He stopped her with a look when she would have interrupted to argue with his summation. "You and your son need protection. I can give you that temporarily, but long term you need to be prepared to deal with what life throws your way. This ain't a perfect world, lady."

Rachel exhaled, forcing her frustration back to a controllable level. "Fine," she acquiesced. "You're right. I need to know how to defend myself and Josh." She lifted her gaze to his. "You can teach me how to do that while we're here?"

He shrugged. "You wanted a plan. That's the plan."

Annoyed by his attitude, she glowered at him. "Is this going to cost extra?"

"I'll throw this part in for free." Sloan turned and walked toward the door. "You'll find what you need to wear for today's lesson in the other room." He paused at the door. "Put the swimsuit on under your clothes and be in the kitchen in twenty minutes."

The man might be barbaric in his manners, but Rachel refused to forget hers. He was doing her a tremendous favor, and she owed him her gratitude, even if she momentarily forgot at times when he made her so angry. Taking care of her the way he did last night wasn't part of the bargain. "Thank you," she offered before he could disappear through the door.

Sloan turned back to her. "For what?"

Rachel moistened her lips and summoned the courage to say what needed to be said. "For taking care of me last night. That was above and beyond the call of duty. I appreciate that you didn't take advantage of me."

Something changed in his eyes. Something Rachel couldn't quite identify.

"You were exhausted, not to mention out of it," he explained. "When I have you, you'll be very much aware of what's happening."

When, not if. Anger washed over Rachel. "That's comforting," she retorted, her irritation building once more. She wouldn't bother to tell him that he could wait until hell froze over and she still wouldn't allow him to seduce her. She had been a fool once. And it would never happen again. Dangerous men—men in general truthfully—were not to be trusted. "After that remark about my ending up in your bed," she added quickly, "I only meant that when I woke up I wasn't sure if…" Her voice trailed off at the renewed intensity in those fierce blue eyes.

The barest hint of a smile tilted one corner of his mouth. "Last night isn't what I meant when I said you would end up in my bed."

With that warning he disappeared down the hall.

Rachel fumed. She would just see about that. Maybe Sloan was accustomed to having any woman he decided he wanted, but she wasn't *any* woman. She had a son to think of. This was a business deal, nothing more.

Never again would she fall victim to any man's charm, no matter if this particular man stirred some restless feeling deep inside her. She had come here for Josh's sake. If she was lucky, when she returned to New Orleans, Angel would be dead. She knew with complete certainty that Sloan understood what she wanted. She wanted Angel out of Josh's life forever.

She wanted him dead.

In that crystalline moment, Rachel acknowledged mentally that she would do anything necessary to ensure her son's future safety. She considered the man in whose home she now resided, then the wide inviting bed which belonged to him. She drew in a shaky breath and released it slowly. Could she do that if he pressed the issue? Angel had been her first, and there hadn't been anyone since. Her judgment was obviously flawed. How could she trust her instincts? How could she bring herself to allow another man's touch?

Rachel frowned when an old memory filtered through her thoughts. There had been a man once who seemed awfully nice, but, of course, she hadn't been interested. Not really. It was about a year and a half ago, before she and Josh had moved to New Orleans. The man had been their neighbor. He was a widower, and seemed as lonely as Rachel. He had dropped by a couple of times and brought fresh bread from the bakery he owned in town. And she had enjoyed the companionship of his short visits. Her frown deepened. But he died only a couple of months after she and Josh moved there. A car accident of some sort.

A chill raced up Rachel's spine. Not once in all this time had she considered that Angel might have had something to do with his death. But now, out of nowhere, the revelation broadsided her. And she knew as surely as she knew her own name, that it was so. Angel watched every move she made.

Just like now.

And, just like Sloan said, he would come. For her. And for Josh.

None of them were safe.

SLOAN GLANCED AT the clock on the wall once more as he poured the freshly brewed coffee into a mug. Rachel Larson's twenty minutes were up. Where the hell was she? He placed the carafe back onto the warming plate, and then the mug onto the table. Patience was not one of his virtues. He hated to wait. Especially unnecessarily. This woman had come to him for help. She would have to learn that it was his way or no way.

Irritated beyond reason, he strode out of the kitchen and in the direction of his bedroom. He slowed in the hall long enough to check and adjust the thermostat as he passed. The previous night's unseasonably cool temperatures had waned, and the wilting August heat had taken its place.

His bedroom was empty. Sloan crossed the room to close the windows since the air-conditioning had just kicked on. He had already closed the other windows Pablo had raised last night to allow the cool desert air to filter through the house. But he had left these open to keep from disturbing Rachel this morning. She had needed the rest.

The bed was made, he noticed when he turned around. His T-shirt was neatly folded and lying atop one pillow. The one she had slept against last night. He picked up the T-shirt and held it to his face to inhale her scent. His groin tightened when her sweet fragrance filled his nostrils. He closed his eyes and allowed the memory of holding her in his arms while he sat on the bedside undressing her to replay. The sandals had been the first to go. After releasing the button and lowering the zipper, he had dragged the long, silky skirt from under her and then down her legs. Her skin had felt like satin beneath his callused palms.

By the time he released the final button of her blouse, he was painfully aroused. Sloan opened his eyes and stared out the window, seeing nothing but the image of the woman who had been in his arms last night. Even now the memory of seeing her small breasts made him hard. It had taken almost more restraint than he possessed not to touch her. Her nipples had tightened into tempting, rose-colored peaks, as if even in sleep her body responded to his touch.

He hadn't wanted to cover her, but he had. His fingers fisted in the soft cotton of the T-shirt that had just minutes ago covered her slim body. He could have carried her to the bed where her son slept, but he hadn't wanted to see the child. He had watched his own son sleep so many nights after a long day at the Colby Agency. Those moments alone with his son had been one of his favorite times. So much innocence. How could anything bad ever touch that sweetness?

But it had. Sloan had brought that evil into their lives.

He repressed the painful memory. That was a long time ago. He would not think about the past today.

The images beyond the window slowly came into focus, bringing Sloan back to the here and now. Rachel needed him and he couldn't turn his back on her. No matter that each time he looked at her son the agony he had spent seven long years burying was resurrected. As Sloan watched, Rachel, wearing the T-shirt and sweats Pablo had selected, knelt before her son and threw her arms around him and hugged him tight. She drew back and brushed the tousled hair from his face and kissed his nose. Sloan turned away.

He had to keep the past out of the present. Remaining focused would be impossible if he allowed those demons to escape the tightly compartmentalized place he had banished them to all those years ago. Sloan thought briefly of Victoria. His life then, his work with the agency seemed so far away. Almost like someone else's history. Victoria had sent this woman to him, Sloan owed it to Victoria to do what he could. She, of all people, understood this level of urgency.

He owed it to himself to take Angel down.

The concept of intense physical training during Rachel's stay here had been borne of necessity. In her current condition, Rachel was as helpless as Josh when it came to defending herself. She needed to build up her strength and endurance, otherwise she would only be a liability when Angel showed up. That wasn't really the issue here. Sloan would deal with Angel.

But until that time came Sloan needed a distraction, or else he would lose what was left of his mind, then he would be a liability…

Just like before.

SLOAN WAS WAITING in the kitchen leaning against the counter when Rachel, breathless from a few minutes of play with Josh, rushed through the door a full fifteen minutes later than he had instructed.

"Ten-thirty means ten-thirty, Miss Larson. This isn't Club Med, and playtime with the kiddies is not on the agenda."

He was PO'd. Impatience and irritation radiated from

him like heat rising off that long stretch of desert high-
way she had traveled by bus from Chihuahua to Florescitaf. He clearly resented her choosing Josh over his
orders. His sandy-colored hair was pulled back, re-
vealing the lines and angles of his handsome face.

"I'm sorry," she offered. "I wanted to check on
Josh."

"Pablo will see to your son while you're training."

Rachel started to argue, then thought better of it. No
point in antagonizing the man the first day. "I'll remember that," she promised. "But *you* will have to
remember that I can't pretend my son isn't here," she
added, intending to make her point whether she argued
or not.

Ignoring her last statement, Sloan gestured to the
table. "Coffee or water." Both sat on the table, ready
to be consumed. "You can eat after this morning's
workout. Tomorrow we'll start at six in the morning."

Six o'clock? Trying not to grimace, she pulled out
a chair and sat down. Choosing the water over the coffee, Rachel took a long sip. "What're we going to do
first?" she asked in hopes of making conversation.
Anything was better than his brooding silence.

His gaze intent on hers, he pulled out the chair directly across from her and straddled it, then propped
his arms across its back. "We'll do some stretches, run
a couple of miles, then do laps in the pool. Maybe
throw in some strength training."

Rachel's eyes widened in disbelief. "Anything
else?" At least she now knew why he'd insisted she
wear the swimsuit beneath her clothes.

"Not until this afternoon." He eyed her skeptically,
no doubt watching for some sign of surrender to the
challenge he lay before her.

She mustered a smile. "Sounds doable." She downed the last of her water and pushed out of her chair, the legs scraping across the floor with her movement. "I'm ready." She tried desperately to remember if she had ever purposely run two miles in her life. She didn't think so. But she would never let him suspect.

Sloan stood in one fluid motion, drawing her attention. He turned the chair around and pushed it beneath the table. A little hitch interrupted her breathing. How could a man as tall and solidly built move so effortlessly? And why did she have to notice?

"Let's get started."

Rachel followed him outside. She waved to Josh who was helping Pablo attend to the pool. "He can't swim!" she called out nervously. Though she felt sure Josh was in good hands, still, he had been to a pool only a few times in his short life, and never without her to watch him.

"Don't worry, *señora*. We'll have him swimming in no time at all."

Josh punctuated the statement with enthusiastic whoops. Rachel smiled in spite of her misgivings. Her son was enjoying himself and that was all that mattered. She had been so afraid that coming here would be hard on him. Pablo was a blessing.

When she directed her attention back to Sloan he was already on the other side of the courtyard, leaving her behind. She hurried to catch up with him, but he didn't seem to notice. He led the way to an atrium that made up a large portion of the west side of the house. The room and plants were gorgeous. Rachel thought again how out of character this house was when compared to its owner. She suddenly recalled his words when she had asked him if he lived here. *Ever since I ran off the local drug lord.* Was it possible that Sloan had been serious?

Now that she thought about it, the place did look like the kind of luxurious setup a drug lord would flaunt, not to mention the elaborate security system.

"How long did you say you had lived here?" She hastened her step to match his.

"I didn't." He kept walking without sparing her so much as a glance.

"Did you design the house yourself?" she persisted. "The layout is spectacular."

He shot her a sideways glance and exhaled impatiently. "No."

So much for small talk. Rachel huffed a sigh of her own. She supposed she would simply have to get used to his ways. Lord knew she was definitely at his mercy.

He passed through another door and Rachel found herself in a room filled with workout equipment. Through the windows on the other side of the room she could see the water tower that stood midway between the house and the protective wall a hundred or so feet away. This was the first time she had seen the back of the property, though she really couldn't see that much. Beyond the wall the beautiful mountains stood proudly in the distance.

"There won't be any distractions here," he said, drawing her attention back to him.

His comment had nothing to do with the view she had been admiring. He meant Josh. He didn't want her son around. Rachel wished she could say something that would make things less difficult. But she couldn't. Josh was Angel's son. Angel murdered Sloan's son. There was no way to paint a pretty picture. Sloan would merely tolerate Josh while they were here.

She met his watchful gaze. "I'm ready. What do you want me to do first?"

Sloan dragged two large blue workout mats to the far side of the room. He stepped onto one and waited until Rachel moved to the other.

"Stretches."

Rachel watched his slow, sinuous moves, then mimicked each as best she could. She repeated each step until he went on to something else and she followed suit. When the stretches were behind them, they set into a routine of exercises, some involving the elaborate equipment that quickly stole her breath. Refusing to give up, she completed the same amount of repetitions as Sloan. But she was pretty sure he had noticed and was adjusting his usual routine to accommodate her.

The two-mile run came next. Rachel couldn't begin to keep up with Sloan's long legs. She was grateful when he slowed his pace so that she didn't lag so far behind. The sun had risen high in the sky by the time they headed back into the house. She had long since lost count of the number of times they had circled the huge compound. Her legs felt like limp noodles. The only scenery was the incredible view of the mountains in the distance beyond Sloan's property.

Sweat rolled down between her breasts as they slowed to a walk when they neared the rear entrance. Sloan wasn't even winded. Rachel huffed like she had run twenty miles instead of two. Sloan continued in silence as he led her back through the atrium and into the inner courtyard. He hadn't paid much attention to her since they started, unless it was to bark an order or to point out a snake basking in the sun on a nearby rock. Rachel wasn't sure if he had done so to warn her or simply to keep her close. No way was she falling far behind when snakes and lizards abounded in the area. Too bad the gate didn't keep them out too.

Just one more thing to worry about Josh coming into contact with. Snakes. She shuddered. She would be sure and mention her worry to Pablo.

Josh and Pablo were having lunch on the patio. Rachel gave her son a quick pat on the head before following Sloan to the pool. Her pulse tripped when Sloan peeled off his T-shirt, tossed it aside, then stripped off his sweats. His running shoes and socks lay next to his discarded shirt. Rachel's mouth went dry as her eyes took in his sculpted body in the brief, snug-fitting swimwear. She blinked and he was gone. The water barely splashed as he cut through the sparkling surface.

Rachel quickly toed off her shoes and dispatched her clothes. Rather than diving in as Sloan had, she took the steps. The water felt wonderful closing in around her heated body.

Sloan stopped long enough to push the damp hair from his eyes. "See if you can manage ten." He turned into his second lap without waiting for her reply.

She couldn't remember the last time she had been swimming, but she had every intention of giving his demand her best effort. Rachel dived into the water and swam half the length of the pool beneath its refreshing surface to cool off. It felt wonderful. How nice it was, she decided as she cut through the water, to have such an amenity in the middle of the desert.

By the time she managed lap number nine, Rachel felt certain she would die right then and there.

Sloan sat on the edge, his damp hair slicked back and curling around his nape. The golden hair sprinkled on his chest glistening in the sun. "You can stop anytime, you know," he offered, obviously reading the strain on her face. "Ten laps was only a suggestion."

"One more," she said between gritted teeth. Her arms moved awkwardly now. But she had to make just one more lap. She would not show weakness. She had to do it.

"Mommy, Mommy, can I swim too?"

Rachel kicked harder to make it the last few feet. She stopped in the waist-deep water and held on to the side of the pool to stay upright. Her muscles quivered in protest of the workout they had gotten.

"Hey, sweetie." She smiled wanly at her little boy. She glanced at Sloan then, who was busy ignoring the whole situation. "Do you mind?" she asked cautiously.

He stood. "Why should I?" He gave Rachel his back and stalked away.

Rachel watched him disappear inside the house. How could she feel sympathy for such a cold, hard man? But she did. He had lost so much. She and Josh were vivid reminders of just how much. Rachel produced a smile for her son and put thoughts of Sloan out of her weary mind. Nothing was more important than her son.

Chapter Four

"Spread your feet shoulder-width apart."

Rachel moved her feet farther apart and took aim once more. "Like this?"

Sloan walked slowly around her, surveying her stance. If his irritable expression was any indication, she wasn't doing anything right.

"Lock your elbow," he ordered.

She stiffened her arm, her left hand supporting her right at the wrist.

"Now." He moved up beside her. "Close your left eye and look straight down the barrel with your right until you've sighted your target."

She did exactly as he told her. The circles on the silhouette blurred then cleared as she focused on the innermost ring—the bull's-eye.

"Take a deep breath and let it out slowly," he said near her ear.

Rachel shivered and lost her aim on the target. She swore silently, and refocused.

"You can't let anything break your concentration," he warned, noting the subtle change. "Losing focus for one second can mean the difference between living and dying."

She drew in a long breath and let it out a little at a time, forcing her tense muscles to relax.

"Fire!"

Without taking time to think, she pressed the trigger just like he had demonstrated before. The recoil forced her hands upward. Rachel staggered back a step. The explosion echoed against the mountains in the distance.

She turned to her instructor and waited for his appraisal. Sloan stared at the target she had missed entirely and made a dismissive sound.

"Let's try that again."

"I've never fired a gun before," she offered quickly in explanation of her lack of skill.

"I noticed."

Rachel steamed at his indifference. The man could be such a jerk. He had disappeared after this morning's workout. Of course, that wasn't so hard to conceive of when you considered the size of his house. She had played in the pool a while with Josh, then put him down for his nap. She smiled as she considered her son's playful antics in the water. He loved it. Pablo was right. It wouldn't take long to teach him to swim. He took to the water like a little fish.

Sloan hadn't reappeared until Josh was out of the way. It worried Rachel that he harbored such negative feelings toward her son. Maybe negative wasn't the right word. He just didn't want to be around Josh. Though she understood to some extent how he felt, it was difficult. She loved Josh. None of this was his fault. He was innocent. Yet, she supposed looking at him was painful for Sloan. Unfair as that was.

"Your feet still aren't far enough apart," he said gruffly.

Startled back to the present, Rachel gasped when his

left arm closed around her waist. He tucked her hard against his muscular body. His right hand covered her left in support of her firing arm. Still holding her firmly against him, his jaw pressed to her temple, he thrust one jean-clad thigh between her legs and forced her feet farther apart.

"Sight your weapon."

Rachel felt the words rumble from his chest. She tried to slow the pounding in her own chest. She moistened her lips and took another of those slow, deep breaths—for all the good it did. She knew he could feel the rapid rise and fall of her breasts, but she couldn't slow her body's reaction to his nearness.

"Relax, I don't bite," he murmured.

"Do you have to hold me so close?"

"Sight your weapon and fire," he ordered, ignoring her question.

Summoning her determination, Rachel tuned out the many ways he affected her one by one. First, the feel of his hard, male body spooned against hers. Second, the whisper of his breath on her cheek. And then the unmistakable scent that belonged uniquely to him. A fine line of perspiration formed on her forehead as she closed her left eye and focused intently on the silhouette hanging in the distance.

She pulled the trigger. Sloan's strong arm controlled the effect of the recoil, his powerfully built body absorbed the force that rocked her hard against him. Each stimulus she had worked so laboriously to disregard flooded her senses once more.

He released her and started toward the target. "Much better," he allowed.

Lowering her weapon, Rachel swayed, this time from the loss of his arms around her. She attempted

without success to rationalize her physical reaction to
the man. Obviously her tremendous gratitude for his
help was spilling over into other emotions she wasn't
prepared to deal with and certainly shouldn't feel. She
hadn't allowed herself this close to anyone in more
than five years. She swiped her forehead with the back
of her hand and pulled in another of those calming
breaths. Maybe it was need, pure and simple.

Sloan held the silhouette out for her inspection.
"Let's see if you can do that again."

Rachel studied the figure and smiled at the small
hole she had made on the edge of the outermost circle.
Now, if she could just learn to do that without his arms
around her.

"Next time just think about Angel when you set
your sights on that faceless silhouette."

She lifted her gaze to meet his and tried to decipher
the hint of emotion in his eyes. She considered the way
he had emptied the weapon into the first silhouette,
each shot a near perfect bull's-eye.

"Is that what you do?"

That strange understanding passed between them
again. Just like before, in the cantina. He didn't have
to say yes. Rachel read the response in his eyes. He
turned away and made the return journey to the stand.
She watched as he placed the target back into position
in preparation for her next shot. With complete clarity
Rachel knew precisely what drew her to Sloan. It
wasn't just the fact that he could protect Josh and her.
It wasn't even the knowledge that he knew Angel better
than anyone, thus offering the best hope at beating him.
No, that wasn't it at all. The single thread that bound
them even now, so early in their new alliance, was their

mutual hatred for Angel. The desire to make him pay for the pain he had inflicted in their lives.

And he would pay, Rachel felt confident for the first time in five long years.

SLOAN SAT IN THE near darkness on the patio. The lights from the pool cast just a hint of light in his direction, but not enough to disturb his sense of concealment. He stared at the bottle on the table and wondered why he even bothered. Hell it didn't do him any good, no matter how much he drank. The damn nine millimeter lying next to it would do a much better job of putting him out of his misery, but he hadn't been able to do that seven years ago and he couldn't do it now. He moved through each day, doing his job and caring about nothing. But now he had the opportunity to take down the son of a bitch who had destroyed his family. And suddenly everything changed.

His ability to take the edge off his waking nightmare had evidently grown impotent with the arrival of his guests. He clenched his jaw hard against the bitter words he wanted to shout into the dark night. Rachel Larson had waltzed into his life hardly more than twenty-four hours ago and already nothing was the same. He couldn't drown the demons from his past. He couldn't sleep and didn't really care to eat. He only forced himself to do so because it was necessary to survival.

Survival.

He laughed at his misnomer. He wasn't surviving, he was existing. He reached for the bottle, but hesitated. What was the point? Whenever he closed his eyes Rachel would still haunt his dreams, waking as well as sleeping. And then the other memories would

creep in. The betrayal would stab at his battered heart
for allowing the son of Gabriel DiCassi into his home.
For allowing the woman who had once been Angel's
lover to enter his dreams at all.

Sloan knew better than to direct any of his rage at
the kid. The kid was innocent, a victim just like him.
He closed his eyes and forced the boy's image from
his mind. He didn't want to know this child, didn't
want to care about him.

Sloan swore under his breath. He was pathetic. His
existence was pathetic. But something so deep inside
him that he couldn't touch it and he sure as hell
couldn't name it, urged him to keep going…wouldn't
let him quit.

He picked up the tequila bottle with the intention of
giving those demons a run for their money anyway
when something in his peripheral vision snagged his
attention. A movement near the pool. Adrenaline
surged through his veins, sending every nerve ending
on alert. Sloan slowly placed the unopened bottle back
on the table. He picked up thc Beretta as he silently
stood and started in the direction of the pool. He stayed
near the edge of the light's reach, cloaking himself in
the concealing darkness.

Taking the weapon off safety, Sloan prepared to
move around the wall of foliage. He listened intently
for any sound. Nothing. He considered only for one
moment the possibility that he had imagined the movement. He had seen it all right. Someone or something
was out there. It wouldn't be Pablo, he was gone for
the evening. Rachel and her son had gone to bed an
hour ago.

Sloan slipped between two large potted plants. The
lights shimmered off the water at the shallow end of

the pool. He inched closer, then swung around the palm tree into the open area around the pool, his weapon leveled on the first thing that made a move.

Josh.

Sloan's hand shook as he lowered the weapon. His body weak with receding adrenaline, he set the safety. It wasn't until that definitive click that Josh looked up from his position near the edge of the pool.

"I founded my bear." He displayed the stuffed animal to back up his announcement, then smiled unsuspectingly up at Sloan. "He was lost."

A harsh breath shuddered from Sloan's lungs. Dammit, he could have—

He forced the thought away.

"What are you doing out here, kid?" He forced his body to relax from its battle-ready posture.

Those big dark eyes blinked at his brusque tone. "I waked up and couldn't find my bear." He hugged the toy close. "My mommy was in the baf'tub...so I comed to look for my bear."

Sloan glanced at the French doors leading to the room Rachel and her son occupied, one door stood open. He swore. Josh's eyes grew even rounder.

"Mommy'll wash your mouth with soap." He nodded knowingly.

Sloan heaved another heavy breath. He motioned for the kid to stand up. "Come on, I'll take you to your mother."

Josh gazed longingly at the pool, then back up at Sloan. "We can't go swimmin'?"

Sloan shook his head. "You can talk to your mother about that. Let's go."

Josh scrambled to his feet, his bear wrapped in one arm. He looked at the weapon in Sloan's hand, then at

Sloan. ''You want t'play army? I could play wif your gun.''

''This isn't a toy,'' he explained. Sloan nodded toward the house. ''Come on, kid, it's late.''

Josh obeyed. Sloan scrubbed a hand over his face and tried to calm his racing heart. The thought of what could have happened throbbed inside his head. He had never once fired a weapon without identifying the target first, but he was edgy. It could happen. It wasn't impossible. The woman would just have to keep a better watch on her kid. Sloan glanced at the boy. Wearing nothing but a T-shirt and his underwear, it was obvious he had been in bed. Why the hell didn't Rachel have the door locked?

The kid suddenly stopped and peered up at Sloan. ''If you had a little boy, mister, then I could play army wif him.''

A chunk of ice formed in Sloan's stomach. If he had a little boy...

RACHEL TOWEL-DRIED her hair and then studied her reflection as she brushed it. The huge tub full of hot water had felt great to her sore muscles. She would be surprised if she could move come morning. Sloan had really pushed her hard today.

Or maybe she had pushed herself. She examined the details of her reflection in the mirror. Not failing was extremely important to her, especially where he was concerned. She wanted to please him, and she couldn't fully understand that. His approval shouldn't mean nearly so much to her.

Rachel's gaze lowered to her nude body. He had undressed her last night. She swallowed, and couldn't help but wonder what he thought of her body. Were her small breasts a disappointment to him? Men like him probably liked full, voluptuous breasts. And she was too skinny, even she recognized that. She was fairly tall, about five-seven. She wasn't blond, she wasn't beautiful or big breasted. Then there was the cesarean scar.

Rachel sighed.

What the man thought of her in that respect shouldn't matter to her. She wasn't here to improve her social life.

Rachel laughed at that one. What social life? She hadn't had one in nearly half a decade. Hadn't been kissed, or touched intimately, by a man in the same. Her body trembled at the sudden memory of Sloan's powerful arms around her. She closed her eyes and enjoyed the warmth that being near him usually elicited. She had to be losing her mind to allow a man so dangerous to make her feel so…needy.

"Enough, Rachel," she scolded. She snatched up her panties and tugged them on. The only thing she should feel for Sloan was fear. And respect, she amended. It took a great deal of courage for him to face this nightmare again, and she knew that. She would have to be a fool not to. But no amount of admiration or gratitude should send her hormones into hyperactivity.

She slipped into her gown. The cool, silky material felt heavenly against her skin. Rachel took a deep breath and stared at her reflection in the mirror. "Sloan is not the kind of man you fall in love with. This is a business arrangement…not a lovers' liaison."

With that declaration firmly resounding in her ears, she padded back into the bedroom to check on her sleeping child. Josh had worn himself out chasing

Pablo's shiny red ball this evening. The man's patience was never ending.

The bed was empty. Rachel's heart slammed against her rib cage. "Josh?" The sound leaked out of her with the air in her lungs. She turned all the way around in the room. "Josh!" Was he hiding? Had he awakened and decided to play—

The door to the courtyard stood open. Fear snaked around her chest and squeezed.

The pool.

Her feet had taken her out the door before the rest of her realized she was moving. "Josh!"

How could she have been so careless? Did she forget to lock the door? What if...

Rachel trembled, then dragged in a gulp of air. He had to be here. He had to be all right. "Josh!" she screamed again.

"Mommy!"

She raced in the direction of her son's voice. He was hugging his bear, walking toward her from the direction of the pool. Sloan was with him, his gun in his hand.

A new kind of fear saturated her senses. He would never harm her son...would he? Rachel's gaze locked on Josh. Those dark eyes, the dark hair, the shape of his face. He looked so very much like his father. Rage boiled up inside her.

Without another hesitation she flew to her child and scooped him up in her arms. "What are you doing?" she demanded, her fury aimed at Sloan. The idea that he would go near her son with a gun in his hand shook her to the very core of her being. He was still wearing the shoulder holster. Why wasn't the gun holstered?

"Are you insane? Why do you have that gun in your hand?"

Clearly confused, Sloan looked from her to his gun and back. "What the hell are you talking about? Why weren't you watching your kid?" he countered as he holstered the weapon.

Rachel held Josh closer to her chest. "I don't want to talk about this now." She glowered up at Sloan. "I'll be back in two minutes, and then we'll talk."

"Fine." Fury snapping in his eyes, Sloan pivoted and strode away. Rachel took Josh back to their room and tucked him into bed. She tamped down the anger Sloan's actions fueled. She would not allow her son to be touched by her irritation with the man.

"Why on earth did you go outside, sweetie?" She smoothed the hair from his cherub face. "You should never go outside without Mommy or Mr. Pablo. I couldn't bear it if anything happened to you."

"I'm a big boy," he insisted. "I hadda find my bear. I forgotted him by the pool." His little lips curled down into a frown. "I couldn't play army. I didn't have a gun." He sighed a sleepy sound. "He wouldn't let me go swimmin' or play wif his gun. He said I hadda ask you first."

Ire rushed through Rachel, but she restrained the outburst that threatened. She would finish her business with Sloan shortly. "He's right," she told her son. Though she hated to admit it. "I don't want you playing with guns and you should never go to the pool without my permission. Promise Mommy that you will never do that again."

He sniffed. "Promise," he murmured.

She smiled and gave him a quick peck on the soft

cheek. "Good. Now, it's way past time for little boys—and big boys," she amended, "to be asleep."

"Night, Mommy." Josh turned on his side and hugged his bear to his chest.

The memory of where the bear had come from still stirred uneasiness within her. But Josh had made the stuffed animal his new favorite toy. Rachel patted him softly and murmured, "Good night, sweetie." She watched him a moment longer, then pushed to her feet. Her anger renewed itself as she walked as quietly as possible to the door. She closed it carefully behind her and then stormed across the courtyard to where Sloan waited.

Sloan leaned casually against an ornate column that supported the part of the roof that canopied a large area near the French doors leading into the main hall. His expression revealed nothing. Right now Rachel was too annoyed to care what he thought.

"What do you mean carrying an unholstered weapon around Josh?" she demanded, hands on hips.

He straightened. Rachel resisted the urge to take a step back. He cocked one eyebrow and glared down at her. "You should keep closer tabs on your kid. If I hadn't seen him, he'd be face down in the pool about now."

Anxiety tightened in Rachel's chest at the image his words evoked, but did little to assuage her fury. "What were you doing with the gun?" she insisted.

"I thought we'd been invaded by aliens and I went to check it out. What the hell do you think I was doing with it when I saw movement in the dark?"

A new kind of terror swelled inside her. "You..." She shook her head, unable to voice the unthinkable. She gathered her courage around her and fixed her gaze on his. "Don't ever take that gun out around my son again."

"It's pretty difficult to protect someone without a weapon." He straightened. "What did you come here for, *Miss Larson,* a protector or a baby-sitter? I'm no nanny."

She blinked back the tears stinging her eyes. God, she hated to cry, but she always cried when she was angry. "Surely you can tell the difference between an intruder and a child!"

"I never discharge my weapon unless I have the target in sight. When I realized it was the kid, I lowered my weapon." He stepped intimidatingly closer. "Contrary to what you appear to believe, I know what I'm doing."

"You actually pointed that thing at my son?" The mixture of fear and anger overwhelmed her then, made her tremble. All other thought ceased. "Just stay away from him." Her voice didn't waver, despite the trembling rampant in her body now.

Renewed anger kindled in that cold blue gaze. "Keep the kid out of my way and we won't have a problem."

"His name is Josh." Rachel took the step of aggression this time. "Little boys are naturally curious. I can't promise you that he'll stay quiet and out of the way. Children play, children explore," she argued, her voice growing higher with each word.

He was truly furious now. His eyes shone with it, his posture shouted it. "I'm surprised you haven't lost him already the way you let him run around here. There are a dozen hazards for kids around this place, besides the damned pool. What were you thinking leaving the door unlocked like that? You can lose your kid in the blink of an eye.''

"The way you lost yours?"

The moment the words left her mouth Rachel knew she had made a mistake. Overstepped her bounds. Her anger died an instant death. All emotion drained from Sloan's expression, from his eyes. The look of devastation that remained ripped her heart into shreds.

"Yes," he said, the word an expression of pain. "Exactly like that."

A tear rolled past Rachel's lashes and trickled down her cheek before she could swipe it away. "I'm sorry," she said tautly. "That was uncalled for. What happened to your son wasn't your fault."

"That's where you're wrong. It was entirely my fault. I made a mistake." His gaze leveled on hers. "Don't make the same one I did."

He turned from her then. More tears trekked down her cheeks, but she didn't care. She was wrong. She had no right to say such hurtful words.

"Wait." Rachel touched his arm, he hesitated, but didn't look back. "You can't believe what happened was your fault." Her fingers tightened on his muscular arm to relay the sincerity of her words. "It was Angel—not you. You didn't do anything wrong."

He turned back to her then, his eyes on fire with some emotion she couldn't quite define. His fingers encircled her wrist and pulled her close. He glared down at her. "You don't have a clue what I've done wrong in my life. All your misguided sympathy isn't going to change the past, so don't waste it on me." His grip tightened. "I don't need your pity, lady. If that's all you've got to offer you'd better go inside and see after your kid."

Rachel jerked free of his hold and glared at him. "Go to hell, Sloan," she snapped.

"I'm already there, or hadn't you noticed?"

Knowing the truth in his words, but unable to bear his indifference, Rachel hurried back to her room.

To Josh.

Chapter Five

Time proved no ally to Sloan in the matter of his houseguests, or his work. By Thursday he still had no leads on Angel's current whereabouts. Sloan could not connect him to any recent assassinations in the States. Things had apparently gotten too hot for him since the Larson hit to risk high-profile assignments in the good old U.S. of A. The bastard was probably doing most of his dirty work abroad these days.

Sloan blew out a breath of frustration. As was now his habit, the house was quiet for a long time before he came inside for the night. Even in this twenty thousand square foot home he felt crowded with Rachel and her son scurrying about. They had only been here three days and four nights, and it felt far too long already. Their presence disturbed him in ways he couldn't or didn't want to name. Pablo appeared determined to make an affair of preparing and serving dinner to the two. So Sloan ate alone, after the others had left the kitchen. Tonight he had skipped the affair altogether. Instead, he sat in his office, staring at a blank computer screen.

He glanced at the near empty bottle on the desk and released a disgusted breath. It was a sad state of existence when that much tequila couldn't even begin to put him out of his misery. He had attempted to methodically numb himself to the desires of his body and the memories he'd just as soon not recall. When that failed, he decided on something else with which to occupy his rambling mind. Research. He needed to know how Angel always found her so easily. Rachel wasn't a stupid person. She had likely taken steps to elude the bastard.

Anything was better than allowing the words she had said to him the other night to replay in his head. *The way you lost yours?... What happened to your son wasn't your fault.*

But it was.

And nothing could change that.

Pushing all else aside, Sloan entered Rachel Larson's name and social security number, which he easily found in her purse, into the Colby Agency system and waited. Victoria continued to authorize his use of her data banks. Hell, he had helped put it together. It wasn't like she could have kept him out. He smiled when he considered his longtime friend. Maybe when he had his head on a little straighter he would give her a call.

Sloan quickly dismissed that idea. His days at the agency were just another part of his past he had worked hard to forget. No point in digging up bones better left alone.

A few minutes later Rachel Larson's life story appeared on the screen before him. The agency ran a thorough background search on all prospective clients. Though Victoria had sent Rachel to him, she would still be investigated. If anything suspicious had been discovered, Sloan would have gotten a call immediately, alerting him before Rachel's arrival in Floresci-taf.

His attention focused on the details emanating from the screen. Twenty-four now, Rachel had dropped out of college at nineteen and disappeared from public life. Her father, Colin Larson of the State Department, had been assassinated in his own home a few weeks prior to her disappearance. Sloan could well imagine Angel's motivation for that one. With the kind of security Larson no doubt had, someone on the inside was almost a must. Rachel had been the key to Angel's success. Her statement and alibi had been thoroughly investigated during the weeks following the murder. The case was listed as unsolved. Since her disappearance she apparently supported herself with the huge estate left by her independently wealthy father.

"Bingo," he muttered. That's how Angel kept such close tabs on her all these years. Shaking his head, Sloan stared at Rachel Larson's five-year-old driver's license photo on his computer screen. No matter how careful she had been in her efforts to elude Angel, she had dipped into that bank account whenever necessary and Angel had her. She couldn't have been any less subtle if she had sent him a Christmas card from each new location. Angel had that account wired, and she never suspected a thing.

Still too sober and restless to sleep, Sloan picked up her purse and prowled through it again. A curse hissed past his lips when he found a transaction slip from the International Bank of Mexico in Chihuahua. Rachel had withdrawn a fairly large sum of money the day she arrived. No wonder Angel had found her down here so quickly.

Next, Sloan opened a plain, unmarked envelope that

looked a little worse for wear. He withdrew a handful of dog-eared snapshots and shuffled through them. Rachel and an older man. Her father, he decided on closer inspection. He couldn't reconcile the woman at home in sweats and a T-shirt with this younger version decked out in sequins and pearls at some ritzy social function. In the pictures her smile was wide and mischievous. Those big brown eyes glittered with happiness, as did the matching ones belonging to her father. Her full lips were rosy and so were her cheeks.

Sloan frowned. Now those eyes were weary and underscored with dark circles. Her lips and cheeks were no longer so rosy. Fatigue and fear had long since robbed Rachel Larson of the happiness that once glittered in her eyes. Sloan tucked the pictures back into the envelope, then shoved the contents back into the purse and tossed it aside. Now she was here, in his home, with Angel's son. Her life had taken a terrible twist five years ago. He glanced back at the screen. Josh had been born in St. Luke's Hospital in Arizona. According to the hospital records, there had been complications and a cesarean section had been necessary.

"I'm thirsty."

As if somehow his ruminations had summoned him, Sloan swiveled in his chair to find the boy hovering near his office door. His own son had been able to sneak up on him like that. Their innocence somehow slipped under his acute detection skills. Sloan fought the emotions that warred inside him each time confronted with Rachel's son.

"Where's your mother?"

The boy rubbed his eyes with his fist. "She's too sleepy, she can't wake up."

Perpetually wary, Sloan pushed to his feet and made

the trip from his office to Rachel's room. The kid followed. Sloan paused to check the alarm. It was armed. No way had anyone gotten in without alerting him.

The glow from the adjoining bathroom light cast a slight halo over Rachel's still form when he entered the guest room. She was sleeping soundly. Sloan supposed that today's additional laps in the pool had done her in. Regret trickled through him before he could stop it. He did what he had to do. Aggression wasn't in her nature. He needed her pissed off so she would work harder. If she hated him, that was all the better. This ill-fated attraction he could feel building between them had to be kept under control.

"See," the kid whispered.

Sloan glanced at his expectant face. "You should be asleep too."

The kid shook his head adamantly. "I'm thirsty."

Sloan sighed in frustration. Why couldn't the kid sleep like his mother? He swore under his breath. "Fine," he relented. "I'll get you a drink."

Sloan stalked through the house, flipping lights on as necessary to illuminate the way. He didn't have to look back to know the boy followed him. He flipped one more switch as he passed through the doorway and the kitchen's overhead lights blinked on. He pulled a glass from the cupboard and filled it half full with tap water. He made a mental note to add disposable cups for the bathroom to Pablo's shopping list. Then the kid could get his own drink when he woke up in the middle of the night like this.

He thrust the glass at the boy. "Here."

"Milk, please." Those big, dark eyes full of unhurried expectation mocked Sloan's impatience.

He dashed the water into the sink and plopped the

glass onto the counter. He gritted his teeth against the emotions churning inside him as he reached into the fridge and snagged the container of milk. Holding the door open with his hip, he poured the milk into the glass, then chunked the container back onto a shelf. He kneed the fridge door closed as he held the glass out to the boy waiting patiently less than three feet away.

The kid turned the glass up and gulped down half the contents, leaving a picture-perfect milk mustache.

"Go back to bed when you're finished," Sloan ordered as he left the room. Irritated beyond reason and with his gut tied in a thousand knots, he dropped back into the chair at his desk. He glared at the image of Rachel on the computer screen. "Why the hell did you come looking for me?" he muttered. "I told you I wasn't the right man for this job."

Resigned to his fate, Sloan focused his full attention on the string of words displayed before him.

"That's my mommy."

Sloan jerked at the sound of the kid's voice. Josh walked right up to Sloan and pointed at the image on the screen.

"How'd she get in there?"

"You're supposed—"

"I wanna see," Josh interrupted as he climbed onto Sloan's lap.

Startled, Sloan stared at the kid, unsure what he should do. His first thought was to run like hell. He blinked. But he was a grown man. He wasn't about to run from a kid.

"Mom-mee," he pronounced slowly, pointing to the name printed beneath the picture. "What does that say?" he demanded then, tugging on Sloan's shirt when he failed to answer quickly enough.

"Hair color, brown," Sloan said crossly. What was he supposed to do now?

"Read Mommy's story to me," the child insisted as he settled against Sloan's chest.

At the feel of the small body resting against him, something stirred beneath Sloan's sternum, an unfamiliar tightening making it hard to breathe. "I don't think—"

"Read it to me," he repeated sleepily.

Sloan swallowed hard. One instinct warred with the other. Push him away, hold him closer. He didn't know what to feel.

"'Kay?" The plea was hardly a whisper.

Sloan began to read the words on the screen, leaving out the parts not intended for small ears. He lost himself to the detailed summary that was Rachel Larson's life. Josh snuggled more closely against him, curling into a fetal position, as the information he wouldn't understand or even remember tomorrow unfolded regarding his mother.

Finally, there were no more words to read. An odd silence filled the room. Too many emotions to sort strummed through Sloan. Reluctantly, he lowered his head and looked at the sleeping child in his lap. The memory of holding his own son exactly like this when he would be working late in his home office played through his mind. The sound of his son's young voice, his rambunctious laughter. The smile that could make the worst day feel like the best. Sloan closed his eyes to fight the tears that burned there. He swallowed against the ache building at the back of his throat. His arms instinctively tightened around the small boy cuddled so close to him.

He would gladly give his life for just one more mo-

ment with his son. How could God be so unmerciful
as to allow his child to die, then sentence Sloan to life?
He clenched his jaw as a single tear slipped past his
restraint. He sucked in a harsh breath and blinked rapidly to slow the emotion still brewing, threatening to
make a bigger fool of him than he already was. His
son was dead. He couldn't change that. Couldn't go
back.

He stood, cradling Josh gently against his chest.
Without making a sound he took the child back to his
room and placed him in the bed with his mother. Sloan
stared down at him for a long while after that. He
would not care about this child, he promised himself.
No attachments, no bonds. Sloan would do the only
thing he could for him—he would destroy the evil that
threatened him and his mother. If it was the last thing
he ever did, he would kill Angel.

THEIR ROUTINE HAD fallen into a rhythm of sorts the
past couple of days, in Rachel's opinion. She worked
hard to follow Sloan's instructions to the letter. She
rarely spoke to him unless she needed to question some
instruction she didn't quite understand. Each day when
the morning workout session was complete, Sloan disappeared while Rachel played in the pool with Josh.
Each afternoon she honed her fledgling marksmanship
skills. After the first couple of shots at each session,
Sloan insisted she wear ear protection. He wanted her
to become accustomed to the sound, thus a couple of
shots without the headset.

Rachel was proud of her progress so far. She hadn't
made that bull's-eye yet, but she always hit within the
circles. She could control the recoil better, and her balance. Sloan was right about one thing, it was all in the

way you held yourself. *Think of the weapon as an extension of your body,* he would say. And he was right, technique was everything. She felt tremendously more confident now. It felt good to be able to protect herself, at least to some extent. A few days ago she hadn't even known how to fire a weapon, much less load one.

There had been no indication other than the bear the day she found Sloan that Angel knew her whereabouts. But Rachel knew his method of operation; he would strike when she least expected it. He would come. And she had to be ready.

After dinner each evening Josh watched television for a while and Rachel sketched with a pencil and plain pad of paper. It kept her occupied. Fortunately Sloan had a satellite which picked up Josh's favorite cartoons. Bedtime came early, however. She needed all the rest she could get to keep up with Sloan's demands. He wasn't an easy taskmaster. Especially if he felt she wasn't giving her all. She had already swam at least a dozen extra laps in the pool each day because he wasn't satisfied.

She sighed when she thought of his refusal to join them for dinner. But Pablo made things a great deal more pleasant. His patience with Josh never seemed to end. Each time Rachel considered how strained the atmosphere would be without Pablo, she thanked her lucky stars he was here most of the time. She wondered if he disappeared to his own home late at night.

Rachel sat down on the side of the bed and watched her son sleep. His rosy cheeks and newly tanned skin made her yearn to hug him and kiss him from head to toe just like she did when he was a baby, but that would only wake him. Josh was always ready for naptime after his energetic romp in the pool and leisurely lunch in the kitchen. Considering this morning's rigorous workout, Rachel felt ready for a nap herself. She yawned. It was Friday, surely Sloan would cut her some slack.

Maybe she would rest her eyes for just a few minutes anyway. She was an adult, she didn't have to ask for permission. She had thirty more minutes before she was to meet Sloan in the *gym,* as he called it. She eased down beside her son and snuggled close to his warm little body. She loved him so very much. She couldn't possibly live without him. Her last thought before she drifted off was of how unbearable it must be for Sloan living with the loss of his son.

Hell. He'd said it was hell.

"SEÑORA."

Rachel's eyes fluttered opened as Pablo gently shook her shoulder.

"Señora Larson, Señor Sloan is waiting for you."

Rachel sat up quickly. She checked the clock on the bedside table. 3:00 p.m. She had slept for an entire hour. She raked her fingers through her mussed hair, pushing it back from her face and met Pablo's concerned gaze. Sloan would be royally PO'd. Why hadn't he sent for her sooner?

"I'll be right there," she assured Pablo.

He nodded and scurried away to deliver her message. Rachel scooted off the bed and padded to the adjoining bathroom. She felt groggy after her unintentional power nap. She hadn't slept that long, or that soundly in the middle of the afternoon in ages. After taking care of essential business, she quickly brushed out her hair and straightened her sleep-tousled clothes. She dropped a quick kiss on her still sleeping child's sweet head and hurried from the room.

She had to admit that Sloan had been right about the soreness as she made her way down the long hall. She had worked most of it out. She felt stronger already. When Angel came, and she knew he would, she wanted to be ready. She felt certain that it would take all the courage and strength she could muster to face him. He would be out for blood this time.

Her blood.

And probably Sloan's.

Pablo and Sloan were talking quietly when she reached the great room. They stopped abruptly when she walked in. Rachel felt certain that she and Josh had been the subject of their hushed discussion.

"Josh is still sleeping," she informed Pablo, then looked from one man to the next. Pablo looked downright embarrassed, Sloan looked like he always did—indifferent. They'd been talking about her all right.

"Not to worry, *señora,* I will take very good care of him."

Pablo made her the same promise each day, and he always did just as he said he would. Rachel was immensely grateful for all that he did for her son. Pablo made life with Sloan tolerable.

Rachel smiled her thanks, then turned to Sloan. "I'm ready."

"Today we're going to do something a little different," he said without preamble. Evidently not deeming clarification necessary, he led the way from the room.

Uncertain whether his announcement was good or bad, Rachel followed. She noted again what a strong man Sloan was. Tall, muscular build. Broad, broad shoulders and a lean waist. Cute butt, she thought with a tiny smile. The way his jeans hugged him was…inspiring. Heat flagged her cheeks. She was acting like a silly schoolgirl. She tried to look anywhere but at his well-formed behind as they continued toward the workout room. She never had this kind of reaction to a man. Not even all those years ago to—

Rachel forced that thought away.

A rare, pleasant breeze shifted her hair around her shoulders. The temperature was hot, but not as unbearably so as yesterday, she decided. What kind of woman would it take to please a man like Sloan, she suddenly wondered? Rachel scolded herself mentally for allowing her musings to wander in that direction again, but somehow she simply could not help herself. She had already decided that she wasn't his type—not that she wanted to be. But she felt certain that skinny brunettes were not his playmates of choice. He would be an aggressive lover, she decided. One who would please his partner over and over before he took pleasure himself.

Her pulse reacted to the vivid fantasy that leaped to mind with the thought. Startled by her own musings, Rachel banished the forbidden thoughts and images of the man in front of her. She needed him rightly enough, but not for anything other than the job she had hired him to do.

Rachel frowned as she considered that he still had not named a price to her. She would have to ask him about that later. If she could get him to talk to her. The only words that had passed between them thus far were the orders he snapped.

Sloan paused near the large blue mats where they usually began their morning workout. She hoped he didn't have more of the same planned. She had flexed and contracted every muscle in her body too many times already.

Well maybe not every muscle, she amended as her gaze swept over Sloan's masculine frame once more. The new thought disrupted Rachel's equilibrium. How could she be thinking like that about this man? About any man?

He shrugged off the holster and laid it aside. "Starting today we're going to alternate between weapons training and hand-to-hand defense tactics," he told her in his usual, indifferent tone.

Rachel's frown deepened. She chewed her lower lip a moment as he slid the two mats closer together. "You mean like karate moves or something?" she asked hesitantly.

He studied her for a moment, those piercing blue eyes trying doubly hard to see inside her head. "Do you have a problem with hand-to-hand?"

Yes, she wanted to shout. She didn't need to touch him, or have him touch her anymore than was necessary. Her imagination was already in overdrive.

"No," she said instead. "I just wanted to be sure we were talking about the same thing."

"Good." Sloan braced his legs wide apart and motioned with one long-fingered hand for her to come to him. "Charge me," he instructed.

"W-what?" she stammered. Rachel smoothed her palms over her loose T-shirt. She didn't want to charge him. The outcome surely would not be good. For her.

"Is there something wrong with your hearing today?" he demanded. "I said *charge me.*"

What had put a burr under his saddle? She had noticed his more uncivil than usual mood this morning, but she had hoped it would have worn off by now. She moistened her lips and took a small step, then stalled. "I'm not sure if I understand exactly what you mean," she hedged.

He walked straight up to her, too close. So close she had to back up to keep from being nose to chest with him. Her traitorous body responded immediately to his nearness.

"What's to understand?" He glared down at her. "What do you do when a man comes at you like this?"

She attempted a shrug, but his fierce gaze stopped her. "Run?"

"I would catch you before you got halfway across the room." Sloan blew out a breath of frustration. "You need to know how to put a man down."

Rachel laughed nervously. "I couldn't possibly put you down. You're much…much stronger than me." And bigger, with far too many bulging muscles, she didn't add.

"If you want to learn," he growled, "you'll do what I tell you." He moved back to the far side of the mat and assumed a readied stance. "Now, come at me."

Afraid to comply, but even more afraid not to, for fear of disappointing him, Rachel marched straight up to him as he had done her. "Okay," she began nervously, "What now?"

He rolled his eyes. Impatience evidenced itself in every angle of his face. "Hit me."

Dismayed, it took a moment for words to form. "I can't do that."

He pinned her with that icy gaze. "Do it."

Rachel blinked, uncertain. "Do we really need to do this? Isn't there another way?" Fury blazed in his eyes, sending her back a step.

"Do you want me to help you, or not? You need to

know how to defend yourself. It might save your life sometime. Or maybe your kid's. This isn't a game. Now, *do it*."

Exasperated, Rachel shoved a handful of hair behind her ear and nodded. "All right." He looked ready to pounce on her if she didn't obey. "Where should I hit you?"

"Just swing at me," he growled.

Rachel drew back and aimed her fist at his taut abdomen. Just before she made contact with her target he moved. The next thing Rachel knew she was lying flat on her back on the mat, the wind emptied from her lungs.

He extended his hand toward her. "You've already had your nap." One corner of his grim mouth hitched up in a facsimile of a smile. "Try to stay on your feet this time."

She accepted his hand and pulled up. He'd done that on purpose. She was sure of it. He knew she wasn't ready for a move like that. "I can do better," she said crossly. "You surprised me, that's all." She lifted her chin a notch when doubt clouded his expression. "Shall we try it again?"

"It might help if you acted like you mean it." He cocked his tawny head and studied her stature. "I've seen smaller women than you take down a man larger than me."

Rachel planted her hands on her hips and studied him just as he had her. "You know what they say, the bigger they are the harder they fall."

He stepped intimidatingly nearer. "Put your money where your mouth is, baby," he rasped.

Anger boiled up inside her. "I'm not your baby."

"Your choice." He readied for the next round. "Hit me with your best shot, *Miss Larson.*"

Rachel aimed for his belligerent face this time. He snagged her arm and flipped her onto her back once more. She grimaced as if in real pain from the fall. A flash of concern flitted through his gaze as he offered his hand. Furious, she grabbed his hand with both hers and jerked with all her might. He stumbled, then went down as she rolled in the opposite direction. One muscular leg snagged her before she could move far enough away. She struggled, but he was on top of her too fast.

"Get off me," she ordered, breathless.

He pinned her arms above her head. His glare was deadly. "Make me."

She squirmed in his hold. His heavy body covered hers, trapping her and making her aware of every male contour. "How am I supposed to do that?" Her heart pounded so hard she was sure he could hear it. "I can't imagine how you stay in business with the way you treat your clients," she huffed. "Whatever happened to customer satisfaction?"

"I haven't had an unsatisfied customer yet," he said huskily, something new kindling to life in his eyes, which he promptly blinked away.

Awareness shivered through her, and Rachel had the strangest feeling that his words were more promise than fact. Or threat, depending on how one looked at it.

"Are you going to do something or are we going to lie here all day?"

A new blast of anger shot through her as she considered her limited options. She was trapped, there was nothing she could do. Anxiety suddenly coursed through her veins, adding to the uncertainty mushrooming inside her. She had to do something.

He shifted his weight slightly, Rachel tensed, then reacted. She jerked her right knee up, aiming for his crotch. He twisted his lower body in a protective move, his attention diverted briefly from her face. Rachel bit his left shoulder as hard as she could.

Swearing hotly, he tried to pull away, she followed. He rolled, Rachel in tow. She fought hard, kicking at every opportunity. One hand slipped free of his hold. She grabbed a handful of his hair. Another ear-scorching curse echoed around them. He was on top of her again. This time he was madder than hell. His breath, as ragged as hers, fanned her face. Rage glittered in his eyes, he trembled with the force of it. She could feel it radiating from his tense muscles, especially those that marked him male. Fear, more real than any she had ever felt in his presence, washed over her.

"Let me up," she demanded, her voice quivering with the fear manifesting itself in every fiber of her being.

He shook with the effort of restraint. The battle taking place in his eyes frightened her beyond anything he could have said.

"Please," she whispered when he didn't move. "You're scaring me."

He blinked, clearly rattled. He released her and pushed to his knees. Rachel scooted away from him then, to the other side of the mat.

He swallowed hard, her gaze followed the stiff movement, before the feel of his eyes on her summoned her gaze to his.

"Are you all right?"

She nodded and scrambled to her feet. "If that's

all," she said, going for calm, but falling well short, "I think I'll just go back…" She gestured toward the door, as she backed in that direction. Whatever had just happened, she didn't want to hang around and analyze it.

He stood as she reached the door. Before he could speak again, Rachel spun away and hurried back to the house.

He had lost control there for a minute. Allowed some emotion she couldn't fully analyze to push him too close to the edge. Was his hatred for her growing rather than diminishing? Maybe she had made a mistake in coming here.

Distressed and certain she didn't want to be alone, Rachel went in search of Josh and Pablo. Maybe Sloan was dangerous, she contemplated. Maybe Victoria Colby didn't know him anymore. After what he had been through, Rachel was surprised he hadn't lost his mind long ago.

She slowed to catch her breath. Maybe he had.

She closed her eyes and allowed the last of the fear to drain away. When it was gone, all that remained was the desire elicited by the feel of his body pressed against hers.

Rachel shook her head in defeat. Obviously she was at least a little crazy too.

How could she be drawn to Sloan when he so clearly despised her? *Hormones, Rach,* she told herself. Nothing but proximity and hormones. *You'll get over it.*

Chapter Six

Sloan glanced at his watch, 6:00 a.m. What the hell
was she doing up so early on a Sunday morning? His
gaze shifted back to the courtyard, to Rachel. As he
stood quietly in the open doorway leading from the
hall, he studied the movements of her hands. She sat
at the patio table several feet away, her profile turned
toward him. She appeared so deep in concentration that
she hadn't noticed his presence.

She was drawing. She had been an art major in
school, he remembered from reading her bio. He ruthlessly squashed the other memories that wanted to surface from two nights ago. The feel of Josh in his arms.
He shook his head. He wasn't going there again.

Rachel looked so intent. Her right hand moved
quickly, but with a light touch. Her hair was pulled up
into some sort of loose bundle on top of her head,
leaving her down-turned face unobscured. The delicate
features of her profile were achingly feminine. Her lips
were very full, and with much more color than when
she had first arrived almost a week ago. The sun, as
well as the feeling of security she had gained since her
arrival had brought that same rosy color back to her
cheeks. Though tanned slightly, her skin looked as

smooth and soft as satin. He knew from experience that it would feel very much like satin.

She sat with those unbelievably long legs propped on the table. She wore shorts today, which displayed a fair amount of toned thighs. Sloan licked his dry lips as his gaze traveled from bare feet to the hem of khaki shorts. The tank top hugged her body well. He wondered if her small breasts were unrestrained today as they usually were. He had noticed on more than one occasion the tight peaks, had felt the firm swell against him when their bodies touched during training. For the life of him he couldn't explain why he found those small breasts so damned intriguing. There was absolutely nothing extraordinary about them, except the intense desire with which he wanted to taste them.

Rachel had gained a couple of pounds, which was good. She was eating right. Probably for the first time in a long while. She was still too thin for his liking. But she was strong, emotionally and physically. He had gotten a glimpse of her fierce determination more than once. She wouldn't say die, no matter how hard he pushed her. He had the distinct impression that she would pass out from exhaustion before she would admit defeat. He admired that quality. Hell, truth be told, he admired a lot more than that. He shifted, his jeans suddenly tight with his growing arousal. He cursed himself again. To his infinite irritation he had lost count of the number of times he had been unable to control his thoughts in that direction where she was concerned.

His behavior day before yesterday shamed him still. How could he have gone so far out of control? So many emotions had gotten all twisted inside him. Josh. Rachel. His murdered wife and son. Angel. He couldn't think, he could only react. He knew he hadn't physically hurt her, but he had frightened her. He had wanted to kiss her so badly. Hell, he hadn't wanted simply to kiss her, he had wanted to take her, whether she wanted him or not. The effort required to force himself back under control had been monumental. He let go a heavy breath. There was no excuse for his behavior. He owed her an apology. No, he owed her much more than that.

They had hardly spoken since. She kept her distance. And he hadn't touched her again. Isn't that what he'd wanted?

Suddenly, she looked up, then turned to him. Her breath caught, he saw the quick movement of her breasts as she inhaled sharply. Her tongue darted out to trace the fullness of her slightly parted lips. It was his turn to have difficulty breathing then. He straightened and started toward her. Her gaze traced his body, making him that much harder. He could almost feel the touch of her eyes as she slowly examined his bare chest where his shirt fell open.

"You're up early," he remarked with more nonchalance than he felt as he sat down across the table from her.

She blinked, clearly startled. By his presence or her own wayward thoughts, he couldn't be sure. But there was no way to ignore the way she had looked at him a moment ago or the flush on her cheeks now. The table shook with her sudden move to get her feet off, then underneath it.

When she was settled, her shuttered gaze met his. "I wanted to work on my drawings without any distraction," she admitted hesitantly.

Sloan took a deep resolute breath and leveled his gaze on her wary one. He wasn't a man to mince words. "I owe you an apology. There's no excuse for the way I behaved the past couple of days, especially Friday afternoon. It won't happen again."

Her mouth dropped open, but she quickly snapped it shut. She nodded slowly as if considering his statement. "All right."

"Good." Sloan held out his hand then and her eyes rounded with uncertainty. He wiggled his fingers. "Don't be shy, Miss Larson, let me have a look."

She rubbed at her neck as if only just realizing it ached from staring down at her work for so long. "It's nothing. Just some drawings I started the other night. You wouldn't be interested." She refused to look at him now.

He leaned forward and tugged the pad from her fingers. "Why don't you let me be the judge of that?"

She started to run her fingers through her hair, thought better of it, obviously remembering the way she had it stacked atop her head, then crossed her arms over her tight little breasts. Damn, he wanted to touch her. The desire swelled so swiftly inside him that it overwhelmed all other thought for the space of two beats. Sloan forced his gaze to the pad of paper in his hand. It was a writing tablet. A frown lined his forehead. Definitely not the right kind of pad for drawing.

"I lost my sketch pad on the trip down," she explained quickly as if reading his mind. "I hope you don't mind my using that notebook. Pablo said it would be okay..."

The fear in her eyes annoyed him. Why did she always look at him that way? Except when she thought he was unaware. It was different then. He had seen a glimpse of her own want. But always, always when he looked directly at her, fear replaced all else in those velvety brown depths. Sloan let go the breath he hadn't realized until just then that he'd been holding. He knew he was a hard man, that his words and actions incited fear in most women and men. But after nearly a week with him, she should know that he would never harm her. Well, he supposed his most recent actions had probably lessened her fledgling trust.

"It's fine," he assured her quietly, then lowered his gaze to the pad in his hand. The drawing she had been working on was of Pablo and Josh. She was very good. Her detailing was actually quite excellent. Given the proper tools he was certain she would be a phenomenal artist. He turned back a page. The courtyard. Then another page was her son sleeping. Sloan peered down at the drawing, long and hard. The image of the child sleeping in his arms transposed itself over the image on the page. He hastily turned another page and stared down at the likeness of himself.

"It's not quite finished," she put in quickly, her cheeks flaming redder.

Did she see him that way? he wondered. The grim set of his mouth, the hard expression on his face. Hell, he supposed she did, that was the way he was.

He tossed the pad onto the table. "You're very good." His gaze connected with hers, pride glimmered there.

"Thank you," she murmured. "When I was a little girl, I used to dream about being a famous artist." She smiled, embarrassed that she had said as much out loud.

Sloan could still see the little girl in her now. She was young, too young for an old man, much closer to forty than thirty, to be looking at her this way. But he wasn't dead, and she tripped way more of his triggers than she should.

"You still could be. You're only twenty-four. Lots of people go back to school after having a child."

She moistened those full lips, his groin reacted. "I wanted to...but I could never leave Josh. I couldn't trust anyone." She shook her head. "It was just a dream."

"It's not too late, Rachel." With much hesitation, she met his gaze. "You could still do it. Don't let one mistake hold you back from living the rest of your life."

She shook her head. "I was a fool. My actions cost my father his life."

The picture of her, dressed in sequins and pearls, smiling and hugging her father, loomed large in his mind. "Angel is a professional. He's honed his talent over the years. You couldn't have known his intent. If he hadn't gotten to your father through you, he would have found another way." Sloan leaned forward again, needing to touch her. He wanted her to believe in herself again. "He wouldn't have stopped until he finished the job one way or another."

She closed her eyes and bowed her head. "Why would anyone have hired Angel to kill my father? He never hurt a soul. He was a good man."

"There's your answer." Unable to help himself, he reached across the table and covered her hand with his own. She started to pull away, but didn't. The feel of her skin beneath his fingers made him ache to feel more. "You've heard the saying Good Men Are Hard To Find? There's a reason for that. The bad guys keep taking them down. Your father stood for something or supported something someone else was at odds with, so they took care of the obstacle he represented.''

"He spent days seducing me," she said so softly that he barely heard her, her face still down turned.

She was talking about Angel. Sloan squeezed her hand, urging her to go on.

"He was the most handsome man I had ever seen. I knew he was much too old for me, but that was part of the appeal." She drew in a heavy breath. "He did everything right, as if he knew just what it would take to win me over."

"He did know," Sloan said quietly. "He probably watched you for weeks. He set you up to get what he wanted. What he took from you personally was just a perk."

She looked up then, tears glistening in those wide brown eyes. "How can I ever trust my own judgment again? He didn't just take my innocence—" she swallowed tightly "—he took my trust, my confidence, everything."

He had been right, Sloan thought grimly. Angel had been her first lover. The son of a bitch. "You can get those things back," he assured her. "But you have to earn them. You'll trust yourself again, when you learn to trust others. The same goes for the confidence. It isn't gone, Rachel, it's only cowering behind the fear."

She pushed back from the table and stood abruptly. She shook her head again. "I made a terrible mistake." A tear slid down her cheek. "The sad thing about it is that I can't regret it the way I know I should." She looked at him, emotions warring in her eyes. "If I regret what happened, that means I regret Josh. And I don't." She turned her back, unable to hold his gaze any longer.

Sloan pushed his own chair back and stood. He moved up behind her, trying to comfort her with his nearness. "You're not a bad person for loving your son," he said softly. He closed his eyes against the need to touch her. "Lots of women end up with the wrong man, but they love their children anyway."

She whirled around and glared up at him. "Angel isn't just the wrong man. He's a killer." Her lips trembled. "Look what he did to you. He…he…" She looked away.

Slowly, in spite of his own emotions waging a battle inside him, he reached up with both hands and swiped the tears from her cheeks with the pads of his thumbs. She tilted her face to him then, those sweet lips trembled once more. "How can you stand to look at me, knowing what I did?"

Need so strong welled inside him that he felt certain his heart would fail in his chest. He wanted simultaneously to hold her comfortingly and to take her ruthlessly. Sloan tried to restrain the desire whirling out of control, but he couldn't. He had to taste her. "Because I can't help myself," he murmured. He leaned toward her, his lips yearning to meld with hers. She touched him then. Her soft hands splayed across his bare chest. And he was lost to the fight.

Her lips felt every bit as soft as he had known they would. Her taste was sweet and so very warm. He cradled her head and deepened the kiss. His want was so strong that he had to restrain his savage desire, for fear of hurting her. She moaned beneath his assault, the sound only urging him on. He touched the seam of her lips with the tip of his tongue and she opened. He thrust inside, his body shuddered with need. Her fingers found their way to the sides of his shirt and fisted there, drawing him nearer. He slid one hand down her back and over the swell of her bottom. He pulled her against him, a useless attempt at easing the ache of his throbbing arousal. The feel of her made him crazy to be inside her.

She tried to pull away. Her small palms flattened against his chest and pushed. "Wait," she said between his forceful kisses.

He pulled her mouth back to his and took it hard. She squirmed in his arms. The feel of her body against him only fueling his raging lust. He would not deny himself this pleasure. The need had been building for days. Her body would soon be on fire just like his. The taste of her salty tears jerked him back to reality.

Sloan pulled back as if she had slapped him. She was crying. And he was a bastard. No better than the man who had taken her the first time. He licked the taste of her from his lips and set her safely away from him.

Her hand shook as she wiped her eyes with the back of it. Her mouth was kiss swollen, nearly bruised from his aggression. "I'm sorry, I shouldn't have..."

Just like before, she thought this was her fault. The realization sickened him. He reached to comfort her, but she staggered out of his reach. His entire body hummed with desire. He wanted her, still, so badly he could barely take a breath. She was wrong, she wasn't the fool. He was.

"I have to check on Josh." She pivoted and ran away from him.

Sloan's fists clenched at his sides. Anger and bitterness, fierce and hot filled him, replacing those forbidden feelings. What was he thinking? How could he have allowed himself to kiss her? He had upset her twice now. He had betrayed the memory of his wife and son twofold. Destroyed any trust Rachel might have developed in him or herself. And for what? To satisfy his own selfish needs.

It wouldn't happen again. This was a business arrangement. And, by God, he intended to keep it that way from this point forward.

RACHEL TWISTED THE faucet's handles, then quickly closed the shower door to wait for the water to get hot enough to suit her. Distracted with thoughts of the man who consumed her entire existence now, she peeled off her swimsuit top and dropped it to the floor. She tugged her shorts down and kicked them aside, then did the same with her swimsuit bottom.

Despite the fact that it was Sunday, Sloan had insisted that she run the two miles and do as many laps as she could in the pool. He hadn't mentioned working on the hand-to-hand self-defense training again. She wondered as she took a couple of towels from the linen cabinet if it was because of what happened on Friday.

She stepped into the shower and moaned softly as the hot spray of water pelted her skin. It disturbed her immensely that she couldn't choose between the dangerous man who inspired fear in her and the one who had listened with such care this morning. She moistened her lips. And who had kissed her so passionately. Her heart fluttered at the memory. She had known on some level that his kiss would be like that. His touch made her tremble, but his kiss stole through her every defense.

Rachel slowly massaged the shampoo into her hair, then rinsed. As the foamy water slid over her skin she considered the gentle way he had assured her that it wasn't too late for her dreams to come true. She could still go back to school, he had insisted. But there had been nothing gentle at all about his kiss. He had possessed her with such intensity that she had been mindless with her own need. The horrifying memories from the past had shattered the haze in one heart-wrenching instant. She had made a mistake once, could she risk herself again?

She shivered even now, with the hot, soothing water sluicing over her body. Still, the memory of Sloan's kiss sent heat swirling inside her, made her feel that strange restless sensation again. But she shouldn't feel that way. How could she ever trust any man enough to share her body with him? No matter that she trusted Sloan completely with her life—or as completely as one could—she could never trust him with that part of her. Or, perhaps she simply could not trust herself. His words echoed through her. *You'll trust yourself again when you learn to trust others.* But she couldn't do that, not yet.

Not on that level.

Steam billowed around her as she stepped out of the shower. She wrapped her wet hair in a towel, then used the other to methodically dry her skin. She slipped on a T-shirt and panties and padded back into the quiet bedroom. She smiled at her son, sleeping soundly in their bed. He didn't have a care in the world, and that's the way it should be. She wanted to keep him safe and happy for as long as possible. Careful not to wake him, she sat down on the edge of the bed and worked the towel over her hair to dry it more quickly.

Sloan had hardly spoken two words to her since the incident in the workout room. Then suddenly, this morning he had been so giving emotionally as well as physically, she had been caught off guard. Rachel's hands slowed in their work. Could it be that so much time had passed with her avoiding men in general that her time spent with Sloan was waking her long-slumbering feminine senses? Had she played mother and protector for so long that she had forgotten how it felt to be protected? She sighed, confused. She forced herself to examine the time she had spent with Angel. The mere image of him sickened her. She winced and glanced at her cherished son. At least something good had come of all the loss.

Angel had been attentive, making her feel special that such a handsome, mysterious man would take interest in a naive college girl. Her friends had been envious. She and Angel had only been together twice, both times had proven more experimental for her than passionate. At the time she had wondered what all the fuss was about. Admittedly, though it grieved her now, she had felt attraction and a measure of excitement during their time together. She drew in a deep breath and confessed what she knew to be the truth. The feelings Angel had evoked in her were nothing to compare with what she experienced with Sloan's mere touch.

His kiss had robbed her of her senses, at least momentarily. Fear had made her hesitate. Fear of trusting him so fully. Fear of trusting herself that much. What if she made another mistake. What would it cost her this time?

Was she willing to pay the price? Things were different now. She was older and she had Josh to consider. There would be no more foolish love affairs for Rachel. Her son had suffered enough for her mistake. She would not risk making another one of such proportions.

A light rap on the door startled her from her confusing thoughts. She hurried across the room to open the door before another knock sounded. Not properly dressed for company, she peeked around the edge of the door. It was Pablo.

"*Señora*, you must come to the kitchen," he said quietly. His eyes did not reflect the hushed quality of his words.

"Is something wrong?" Her heart reacted to the concern and fear she saw in his dark eyes.

"I'm afraid so. Señor Sloan says you must come right away."

"I have to change." She started to close the door.

"No, *señora*," he insisted. "You must come *now*."

Fear chilled her insides.

"What about Josh?"

"I'll stay with the boy."

She nodded mutely and opened the door wider for him to enter. Please, God, she prayed, please don't let Angel be here. She wasn't ready.

SLOAN REREAD THE typewritten note in his hand once more. The son of a bitch was playing his game. A note had been left at the front gate. Tied there with a yellow ribbon. The same kind the entire city of Chicago had tied around trees, mailboxes, and lampposts to signify their prayers for Sloan's missing child. Adrenaline rushed through his body again, awakening the demons so that they roared inside him. He clenched his jaw against the explosion of emotions.

He pushed off the counter and plowed his fingers through his hair. He wasn't concerned about going up against Angel. Sloan would win this time. Angel was going to die, one way or another. It was Rachel that worried him. She needed more time. Hell, maybe the time would never be right for her. She wanted Angel dead, yet he was the father of her child. How would she ever explain that to the kid?

As if on cue, she burst into the room. The pale look of dread claiming her features was reason enough to incite him to murderous thoughts where Angel was concerned.

''What's wrong? Pablo said you had to see me right away.'' She searched his face, his eyes for some forewarning of what he was about to say.

Sloan handed her the note. It was the only explanation she would need. He waited silently, knowing her devastation would be complete when the impact of the words he had memorized absorbed into her brain.

> Rachel,
> You have two days to leave Mexico or I'm coming for my son.
>
> Angel

''My, God,'' she choked out. ''He's coming.''

''It looks that way.'' Sloan took the note from her trembling hand.

''Where did it come from?''

Sloan shrugged. ''It was left at the gate. The vehicle was dark, maybe black, a sedan. Probably a rental. I didn't get the plate number.''

''You're sure whoever it was is gone.''

''Positive.''

Rachel's fearful gaze locked on his. ''He knows we're here. What are we going to do? We can't let him take Josh.''

Anger twisted in Sloan's gut at the intensity of her fear. ''He isn't going to take Josh.''

"How can we stop him?" she demanded, the pitch of her voice rising with the hysteria clearly building inside her.

"He won't win this time, Rachel." Sloan grasped her arms and shook her gently. "I won't allow him to harm you or Josh."

Her head swung from side to side in denial. "He'll kill you." She swallowed tightly. "And he'll kill me, then he'll take Josh."

"We have time to react. Trust me."

"You don't understand," she argued. "He's here. How else could he know how to find me? He's coming for my son."

Sloan struggled for calm. "Listen to me, Rachel." He willed her to look at him. She complied. "If Angel were close, he would simply strike. Sending warning messages is not his style. Someone else sent this message. Someone who's doing Angel's baby-sitting."

"I don't understand," she said haltingly. "Who?"

He let go a mighty breath. "That I don't know. A girlfriend maybe. As far as I know, Angel has never had a partner." Sloan considered the events in town the afternoon Rachel tracked him down. "Maybe the woman who gave Josh the bear. Whoever it is, he or she is watching you. They've probably kept Angel up to speed."

She frowned, tears threatening. "Are you saying that the note might be a hoax?"

"I wouldn't risk it. Angel may have instructed his messenger to send it in hopes of avoiding a confrontation with me. He'd rather have you back in New Orleans where it would be just the two of you."

Rachel blinked furiously, but a tear trickled down anyway. "We can't let him find my son," she whispered, her ability to stay vertical in serious jeopardy now.

Sloan pulled her close, sliding his arms protectively around her. "Don't worry, we're going to make sure he doesn't find Josh."

"How can we do that?" Her voice was muffled by his shirt.

"We're going to take him someplace Angel will never think to look."

She drew away from Sloan, searching his eyes once more. "Where?"

"Someplace the rest of the world has forgotten."

Chapter Seven

Following Sloan's instructions, Rachel quickly shoved clothes into the dark, canvas backpack. Satisfied that she had everything she and Josh would need for a couple of days, she dropped the pack to the floor and dressed in the darkest clothing she owned. She rarely wore black. The color was Angel's calling card. He always wore black.

Rachel shivered. Her chest felt so tight she could hardly draw in a breath. But now wasn't the time to think about Angel. His warning echoed inside her head. He was coming for his son very soon. They had to hide some place safe. Sloan would take care of Angel. The prospects of Sloan having to face the man worried her, but it was the only way. To kill a man one had to be willing to face him. And Sloan was willing.

She released a shaky breath. Never in her life had she wanted so badly for someone to die. She prayed Sloan could do the job without getting hurt...or worse. Unless Angel died, she and Josh would never be free. Somewhere beneath all her fear and hatred for the father of her child, Rachel knew it was morally wrong to wish for his death. But, God help her, she just couldn't stop herself.

She tugged on the navy blue tank top, then the black shirt Pablo had provided in case she didn't have anything dark enough. The shirt belonged to Sloan. It was much too large for Pablo's small, thin frame. Rachel smoothed her hand over the soft cotton material. Need welled inside her so fast it made her knees weak. She willed the unbidden yearning back into submission. The unfamiliar feelings he evoked in her confused her as well as frightened her. She shouldn't be experiencing these kinds of feelings. Sloan was not the sort of man a woman fell in love with unless she wanted to get her heart broken. Rachel didn't need any more damage to her heart. The only thing she needed from him was his protection.

After tying her shoes, she gave herself a final once-over in the mirror. The big shirt hung on her like a tent, but it would do the trick. She was as ready as she would ever be. All she had to do now was get Josh ready. Her eyes sought the child sleeping soundly in the rumpled bed. Rachel released a heavy breath. Josh was all that really mattered in all this insanity.

Please, God, she prayed, protect my baby.

She grabbed the dark clothes she had selected for Josh and crossed to the bed. She sat down on the edge of the mattress and gently roused her little boy.

"Josh," she murmured. "Wake up, sweetie, we're going to play hide-and-seek." That was what she always told him. Whenever they had to run, whether it was the middle of the night or straight up noon, she always made it a game. "Come on, sweetie," she encouraged when he curled into a little ball beneath the covers. "We have to hurry. Mr. Sloan is going to play, too. He's waiting for us."

Her son's eyes popped open. He rubbed one with his

fist. "'Kay." Josh scrambled from under the cover. "Can my bear play, too?" He hugged the stuffed animal to his chest.

"Of course your bear can play." Rachel produced a smile. She refused to consider that the damned thing likely came from Angel or whomever he had watching them. She couldn't really be sure, and Josh loved the fuzzy stuffed animal. There was no reason she could think of to make him leave it behind.

Once bathroom necessities were out of the way, she dressed her son as hastily as she had herself. Rachel pulled on the backpack, then reached for Josh. He hugged his arms around her neck and rested his little head against his mommy's chest. She inhaled deeply of his sweet scent and sent up one final silent prayer. Rachel was halfway to the door when the anticipated knock came.

Dressed completely in black, Pablo waited in the hall. "We must hurry, *señora*. I will carry the boy."

Rachel shook her head. "I'll carry him," she insisted. Though she trusted Pablo, she wanted Josh with her.

He nodded reluctantly before turning away. Rachel followed him through the house, then across the quiet courtyard. In the atrium, they took the door leading to the rear of the property as she and Sloan did each day for their run and target practice. Her heart pounded harder with each passing moment. She didn't ask the questions tightening her chest. She had to trust Sloan. Where he was taking them didn't matter. All that mattered now was keeping Josh safe. Pablo paused at the towering wall and entered the code required to open the massive gate. She wondered then where Sloan was. Had he gone ahead of them? That notion unsettled her further. Though Pablo was a good man, Rachel felt much safer with Sloan—at least as far as personal protection went.

A quarter moon provided enough illumination for Rachel to see fairly well. Pablo's short legs ate up the ground before them. Rachel hurried to catch up for fear of losing his wiry frame in the darkness. The order to dress in her darkest clothing was crystal clear to her now. They were less likely to be seen in the dark of night by anyone watching the house.

Rachel suddenly slowed. Why hadn't Sloan joined them? Was he waiting up ahead? She peered at the dark terrain that stretched before her. She could see nothing. She strained to listen. Nothing. Pablo moved forward soundlessly, leaving her behind. She supposed she had better catch up again. But where was Sloan?

"Keep moving."

The quiet order came from right behind her. Rachel spun around to find Sloan only inches away.

"I didn't know you were behind me." She struggled to capture the breath that had escaped her. "I was afraid to go on without you." Her arms tightened instinctively around her son, who had fallen back to sleep the moment he settled into her hold. "Where are we going?"

Even in the sparse light she could see Sloan's vivid eyes. Such a translucent blue, and unnervingly intent. The pounding in her chest increased, but it had nothing to do with what might lay before them. It was Sloan. His presence surrounded her. Though she feared her reaction to him on many levels, anytime he was near, Rachel felt safe. She almost shook her head at the absurdity of her other feelings, but they were there just the same. She felt bewildered by her body's response to him. There simply was no explanation. He was fiercely demanding and forever indifferent to even his own feelings. He defined dangerous. But every part of her longed to know him intimately.

He touched her arm, sending heat rushing through her traitorous body. "Pablo is waiting. I'll carry Josh now."

"I'm fine." Rachel didn't give him a chance to argue the point. The urgency she'd heard in his voice propelled her feet, about the only part of her that was not affected by his nearness, back into action. She hurried in the direction she had last seen Pablo. She squinted, hoping to get a glimpse of movement. Rachel tried not to think about the snakes, or the lizards she knew resided in the area. Goose bumps raised on her skin and she moved a little faster. As scared as she was of the reptiles that might be slithering around her feet, she knew without a doubt that there was nothing in this desert that posed as deadly a threat to her and her son as Angel did. And standing around lusting after Sloan wasn't going to help.

"This way, *señora*."

Startled after several long minutes of total silence, Rachel took a calming breath, then followed the soft sound of Pablo's voice as he repeated his instructions. Sloan was somewhere behind her. Though she didn't look back, she could feel him. She had the impression that he moved around them frequently. Sometimes way ahead, sometimes lagging behind. He was scouting for Angel or his helper, she realized after further consideration. Rachel's skin crawled at the thought that Angel might be out there somewhere. But Sloan had assured her that whoever left the note was gone. She forced the worry away and focused on keeping up with Pablo.

"You must stay very close, *señora*," Pablo warned as she all but collided with him. "The path grows treacherous now."

They had reached the base of the mountains. The rugged peaks that looked so beautiful in the light of day, loomed ominously in the darkness, half hiding the moon. Rachel could feel the change in the terrain beneath her feet. Though still sandy, the ground was more uneven now, the clumps of scrubby grass much thicker and more prevalent.

"I won't fall behind again," Rachel assured Pablo. She didn't want to take any chances that if anyone were out there, they might catch up to them.

"The higher up we go, the more narrow the path becomes," Pablo explained. "Keep to the right, hug the cliffs."

Rachel followed his gesture as he pointed to the vertical terrain rising before them. "Okay." Her voice reflected the anxiety she couldn't restrain. Among her numerous other firsts since her arrival, she had never climbed mountains before. That her first expedition was with only the moon to light her path didn't help.

Sloan's hand was at the small of her back then, urging her forward. She obeyed, moving cautiously. Pablo matched his pace to hers, speeding up when Rachel moved faster, then slowing down as she did. The trail climbed upward, winding around the cliffs, its width cut right out of the face of the mountain. The oak and pine trees that soared amid the mountainous terrain cast long shadows around her, completely darkening the path in places. She couldn't slow long enough to consider the sharp contrast between the forests of the mountains and the meager desert scrub surrounding Sloan's house not so far away.

Rachel kept her gaze steady on her path. She didn't dare look beyond the narrow ledge for fear she would stall dead in her tracks. Her stomach knotted against the butterflies flapping their tiny wings inside her. The skin on the back of her neck prickled against the unseen threat. How much higher would they climb before they started their descent?

Rachel shifted Josh's weight in her arms. She couldn't be sure how long it had been since they left the house, but her arms ached and her legs felt like rubber. One way or another she had to keep going. Pablo was very far ahead of her now. Hastening her step, she stumbled but caught herself before she hit the ground. Josh whimpered and tightened his hold around her neck. Once her heart had slid back down into her chest, she soothed her baby with soft cooing sounds. Trembling with her own unmanageable fears, Rachel forced one foot in front of the other. She couldn't stop now. They had to get as far away as possible. Angel was coming.

Pablo paused until she came up beside him, he reached for Josh then. "Let me carry the boy now, *señora.* You grow weary." Josh resisted, snuggling closer to his mother.

"It's okay," Rachel returned. "I'll manage." Though Josh loved Pablo for a playmate, at naptime or bedtime he wanted his mother.

"He's slowing you down too much," Sloan growled next to her.

Rachel shifted to peer up at him. His posture reflected the impatience in his tone. Pablo reached for Josh again, but he would have no part of it.

"Come on, sweetie," Rachel urged. "Pablo wants

to carry you for a while. Mommy will be right behind you.''

"No!" Josh clung to her.

"I'm sorry," she began, hoping the two men would understand the fears of a child. Though she wanted to comply with Sloan's demands, her son's comfort came first. "He—"

Sloan took Josh from her arms before she could finish her sentence. A wail of protest burst from her son's mouth. Rachel reached for him, but Sloan backed away.

"Keep moving," he ordered.

Josh stared up at him as he spoke. Suddenly, as if only then realizing who held him, he snuggled against Sloan's chest. Stunned, but immensely relieved, Rachel resumed her trek behind Pablo. Her entire body shook with weariness now. Her arms trembled after having carried Josh for so long. But she would have carried him until she dropped from exhaustion if necessary. She glanced over her shoulder once more. Her son clung to Sloan as he had clung to her minutes before. The image warmed her.

"No slowing down, Rachel."

She shivered at the sound of her name on Sloan's lips. He hadn't called her by her first name before. Rachel shook off the foreign sensations and trudged after Pablo. Why should it make her tremble so to hear him call her name? She was tired. That's all. She had no idea what time it was, but she felt certain that physical exhaustion was her problem at the moment.

But what about the rest of the time?

His every touch, every look affected her deeply. She knew it. There was no point in denying the truth. He was her protector, her hero. That's all, she decided. It wasn't personal, it was chemical. As soon as Angel was out of her life and she and Josh returned home, Sloan would be nothing but a distant memory.

One last look over her shoulder was all it took to make a liar out of her. Her gaze connected with his in the moon's silvery glow and fire surged through her veins. Rachel wondered if he felt it too?

She almost laughed out loud at that one. Men like Sloan didn't come undone over a silly hero-worshipping female. She was most likely nothing but a nuisance to him.

"Get the lead out," he barked, confirming her musing.

Rachel sighed and quickened her pace. Just because he had kissed her didn't mean anything…except that she was even more pathetic than she thought.

BY THE TIME they started their descent, Sloan had grown accustomed to the little body clinging to him like a choking vine. This, he thought with self-deprecation, was the very reason he hadn't wanted to take this case. He didn't want to feel anything for Rachel Larson or her son. Despite his best efforts, Sloan was drawn to the boy in a way over which he had no control. The memory of him falling asleep in Sloan's lap the other night haunted him even now. He didn't want to be reminded of how a child's warm little body felt in his arms. Or of the way they slept so innocently, so trustingly. But it was too late now, the deed was done. He cared for the child with the basic human compassion he thought he had buried long ago. And, God forgive him, he hated himself for it. This was not his child…this was Angel's son.

No matter. Sloan had failed to protect his own son,

but he would not fail Josh. Angel would not take Josh from his mother, nor would he harm either of them. Sloan intended to kill the bastard. Very soon. He clenched his jaw against the rage that threatened to overwhelm him. Now was not the time to allow those emotions. Right now he had to concentrate on hiding Josh away from the game that had begun. Sloan's gaze traveled over Rachel as she picked her way downward. Convincing her to leave the boy would not be easy. But it was necessary to the child's safety.

Rachel stumbled again. Sloan tracked her progress as she pulled herself up and continued the difficult journey. Pablo reminded her again to stay to the right. If Rachel paused and took detailed note of the dizzying drop that lay to the left of the goat trail they now descended she would likely faint with fear.

Sloan tightened his hold on Josh and navigated a particularly treacherous, twisting drop. Rousing enough to recognize that he was no longer in his mother's arms, Josh whimpered.

"It's all right," Sloan murmured against his head. He tried not to notice the scent of baby shampoo, but it was impossible. The memory of holding his own son so close when he was frightened exploded into his consciousness. Climbing the big tree in the middle of their backyard with his son zoomed into vivid 3-D focus. They had sat there for hours on end just to watch the birds go about their business. Mark had jabbered about the adventure for days.

Mark.

Sloan hesitated. *His son.* Pain so fierce that his breath ripped through him. He hadn't consciously allowed that name to enter his thoughts in years. Stalling, he closed his eyes and tried to repress the images of his son's sweet face. The thick curls that were more blond than brown. Laughing blue eyes. And a big toothy smile.

Rachel's shriek jerked Sloan from his painful reverie. His heart slammed hard against his sternum. She had stumbled again. The momentum as she slipped to the ground, then slid forward took her the last few feet of the downward trek before Sloan could reach her.

"You okay?"

She stood and dusted herself off. "Yeah. I tripped over something," she said, her voice shaking. "I was trying to catch up with Pablo."

"He went on ahead to announce our arrival."

A brittle laugh slipped from her lips. "No wonder I couldn't catch up with him." She paused, belatedly absorbing his words. "Announce our arrival?"

Sloan ushered her forward. The trail wound to the right and off through the trees now. In fifteen or twenty minutes they would arrive at the small village where Pablo's people lived. The group was reclusive and distrustful of strangers. It was important that Pablo explained their arrival in advance.

"There's a village not far from here," he explained. "Pablo's family lives there."

"Is that where we're going?"

"Yeah." He pushed onward, hoping she would follow without asking any more questions.

There was no need to explain the rest right now. Sloan scanned the sky. He felt a storm brewing. The wind kicked up, making him all the more aware of nature's restlessness around them. There would be no time to waste once Pablo had paved the way for Sloan's plan. He glanced down at the boy sleeping in his arms. The sooner this was done the better off they would all be.

Twenty minutes later a welcoming campfire came into view. Sloan breathed a bit easier upon seeing the dancing flames. The fire was a sign that Pablo's people welcomed the strangers into their village. Had they not been welcome, there would have been darkness and silence. Three figures stood within the light of the flames—Pablo, a woman Sloan recognized as Pablo's elderly mother, and the village leader, Camilo.

Sloan turned to Rachel before they entered the perimeter of the village and lowered Josh into her arms. Later she would have regretted not having held him those final minutes. He hoped she wasn't going to make this any tougher than it needed to be. There was no other way to ensure his safety. Sloan scanned their surroundings as he moved toward the waiting group. The numerous sod huts and primitive cabins fanned out from the village center like the spokes of a wheel. The small party waited in the center, the place of honor, to greet their guests.

A rough male voice uttered a simple phrase that Sloan recognized as a greeting of welcome.

Sloan bowed slightly in deference to the man's village title. *"Gracias."* Though he understood some of the native language used by these people, he spoke none. Pablo would translate.

"Camilo says yes to your request," Pablo said as they approached. "My mother has also agreed."

"Muchas gracias, Señor Camilo," Sloan offered, *"y* Señora Vecino." He placed his hand over his heart to emphasize the depth of his gratitude. Spanish was not lost on these people, and Sloan was aware that any attempt at direct communication would be appreciated.

The elderly woman spouted a short monologue in her primitive language, much too quickly for Sloan to grasp the complete meaning. He turned to Pablo who quickly translated for both Sloan's and Rachel's benefit.

''Mother says that a child is a treasure from God and all measures must be taken to cherish and nurture such a gift.''

Sloan nodded his agreement. *''Sí, señora,''* he bowed again to the elderly woman.

Señora Vecino lifted a small stick of wood from the fire to use as a torch and gestured for them to follow. Sloan guided a hesitant Rachel forward. The woman led them to a nearby hut, somewhat smaller than the others. A dim light marked the low entrance. With a sweep of her hand she indicated that Rachel should enter before her. Rachel's uncertain gaze collided with Sloan's. He nodded for her to obey. Looking entirely too much like a lost child herself, she ducked through the open doorway. Señora Vecino scurried in next. Sloan followed.

Two thick pallets of animal pelts covered most of the available floor space in the main room. Señora Vecino motioned for Rachel to place Josh on one of them. Again Rachel looked to Sloan for assurance. He nodded.

Rachel knelt next to the nearest pallet and carefully laid Josh in the center of it. His lids fluttered open, but quickly closed once more. When it was clear that Josh would continue to sleep, the elderly woman made an urgent sweeping motion with her gnarled hands. She wanted them to leave. Rachel hadn't missed the meaning either. She looked startled and completely bewildered. When Rachel didn't move swiftly enough the

woman mumbled crossly, the words spoken too quickly
and gruffly for Sloan to catch the meaning.

"What is she saying?" Rachel held her ground next
to Josh.

Sloan closed one hand around Rachel's arm and
pulled her to her feet. "Let's talk outside," he whispered near her ear.

She shook her head adamantly. "No. I'm not leaving
Josh."

The old woman grumbled something that sounded
very much like, *"away with you, the devil is on your
heels."* If she only knew how close to right she was.
Too damned close.

"Don't make this anymore difficult than it needs to
be, Rachel," he warned in a low, lethal tone he hoped
relayed the seriousness of the situation.

Tears brimming in her big brown eyes, she followed
him outside. "What do you think you're doing?" She
jerked free of his hold and glared at him. Fear and
worry radiated from those velvety depths.

"He'll be safer here. We have to go back."

She shook her head again. "No way. I won't leave
him." Her chest rose and fell too rapidly. Hysteria
would set in any second now.

She was afraid she would never see her son again.
Of all people, Sloan could sympathize with that heart-
wrenching fear, but there was no alternative.

"Listen to me." He took her by the shoulders and
gave her a little shake to bring her to her senses. "Angel is coming. Maybe not tonight or tomorrow, but
soon. We don't want Josh anywhere around when that
happens. He'll be safer here."

Rachel pounded her fists against his chest as a sob
shook her. She knew he was right, but the pain of leav-

ing her son behind was more than she could bear. "How can you be sure he'll be safe here?" she demanded. Tears rolled down her cheeks, twisting the knot in his gut that much tighter.

"He'll be safe." He wanted to take her in his arms more than he wanted to take his next breath, but that wasn't what she needed now. She needed to think rationally. "These people will hide Josh among their own children. With his coloring no one will ever suspect that he doesn't belong here—even if anyone came looking, which is highly unlikely." Her lower lip trembled and his whole body reacted. He pulled her close and held her in spite of the warnings sounding in his head.

"We've never been apart before," she sobbed against his chest. "I'm not sure I can do it."

The fingers of his right hand threaded into the silky length of her hair as the left splayed on her slender back, holding her body to his. The need he felt could be contained no more. Sloan kissed her temple, then lower, next to her ear. She shivered. "Don't cry," he murmured. "I swear he'll be safe here. Pablo will protect him with his own life."

She tilted her head back, searching out his gaze in the sparse light. "And if we can't come back for him?" She blinked back the fresh wave of tears he heard in her voice. "What happens then?"

He clenched his jaw against the flood of emotions that washed over him. When he had composed himself he leveled his gaze on hers and said the words tightening his throat. "You will be back for him," he promised. "This battle is mine."

She searched his eyes for the truth in his words. "I have your word on that?"

"You have my word."

She swiped the tears from her cheeks with the backs of her hands and drew in a heavy breath. "All right." She pulled out of his arms. "I just need to kiss him goodbye."

Sloan stepped back for her to pass.

Rachel struggled to pull herself together while Sloan said something in Spanish to the old woman who hovered near the door. Rachel's chest ached with every beat of her heart. She held her breath and fought a new rush of tears. She had to be strong. Josh's life depended upon her strength right now. She had Sloan's word that everything would be all right, and she had to trust that. Victoria Colby's statement resounded in her ears. *Someone I would trust with my own life.*

"Don't wake him," Sloan said, drawing Rachel's attention back to him. "There's no point in upsetting the kid. Pablo will be with him when he wakes."

"Sí, señora."

Rachel turned to Pablo who had stepped from the shadows. This all felt too surreal. This place—*a place the rest of the world has forgotten, Sloan had said*—felt too surreal.

"Hurry, Rachel." Sloan ushered her toward the small door. "We have to get back."

Rachel felt confused. Why did they have to hurry? Why couldn't they stay until morning and then she could explain things to Josh. She swallowed with monumental difficulty. Because Angel was coming. He might be there by morning.

The old woman blurted something in the alien language that definitely wasn't entirely Spanish. Another plea for her to hurry, Rachel supposed. Suffering that strange detached feeling again, she ducked her head and stepped back into the rustic hut.

Josh slept soundly, completely oblivious to the life-altering circumstances happening around him. Tears welled in her eyes once more and Rachel cursed herself for being so weak. She knelt beside her baby and kissed his smooth cheek. She brushed the dark hair from his face and smiled, committing to memory once more just how beautiful her child was.

"I love you, Josh," she whispered. Her hand trembled as she caressed his baby soft hair. "Mommy'll be back for you soon. I promise." She kissed him one more time then pushed to her feet and rushed out the door without looking back.

She stood only a few feet from where her baby lay sleeping while Sloan gave Pablo his final instructions. Rachel wanted to scream her agony. She shuddered with the need of it. She scrubbed the tears from her eyes and battled the rampant trembling in her body. She had to do this, she repeated silently. When Angel was dead, she would be back. Sloan had promised.

And Angel would die.

"It's time to go." Sloan took her by the arm and propelled her forward.

Rachel glanced back one last time at the tiny primitive hut where her son slept. No force on earth would keep her from her son.

She would be back.

Chapter Eight

"We need to move quickly, a storm is coming."

Rachel felt numb. Why didn't he just leave her? She faltered in her forward movement, hoping he would do just that. Her feet felt too heavy to lift for the next step. She wanted to go back to the village and cradle her son in her arms.

"We don't want to be caught in the open when it hits," he added, his words meaningless to her.

Not really caring, but knowing that he wanted her to heed his words, Rachel surveyed the sky. As she watched, a dark mass of clouds moved across the moon. The wind was stronger now. Maybe Sloan was right about the weather. She knew little of the weather changes here, and cared even less at the moment. She was too heartsick to worry about trivial issues like the weather. She swallowed, fighting the renewed urge to cry.

How could she leave Josh like that? Reason told her that Sloan was right, he would be safest with Pablo and his people. But reason had never controlled her heart.

"Rachel—" Sloan's deep voice resonated around her, summoning her attention to him once more "—we have to move faster."

Reaching way down deep inside, Rachel found the grit to take another step, then another. When she had reached Sloan, she pushed harder, forcing her feet to cooperate…to take her farther away from her son. Her stomach roiled. Josh would cry when he woke and found her gone. He wouldn't understand that his mommy had left him there for his own good. Tears welled in her eyes, a stinging reminder that she had no choice.

Rachel inhaled deeply of the cool night air. The scent was fresh, earthy. She listened to the sounds around her as she trudged onward. The hoot of an owl, the rustle of the leaves and branches in the wind. She pushed herself to climb more swiftly up the rugged path. Maybe if she ran as fast as she could, pushed her body harder than ever before, maybe then those awful, heart-twisting feelings wouldn't catch up with her again.

Rachel had never left her son before. Not once in his life had she been separated from him. Not even in the hospital when he was born. His bassinet had been in the room with her. Except, she amended, for those few minutes the day she found Sloan. But that was the only time she and Josh had been apart. Would Pablo hold him when he cried? Would he understand the fear that would fill her little boy? Her heart banged painfully, keeping a rhythm of sorts with the words throbbing inside her head. Sloan's rational words joined the others whirling there. Angel would never find Josh. An odd relief flooded her with that last thought. Even if the bastard killed her and Sloan, which was very possible, he would never find Josh.

A smile tugged at the corners of her mouth. Josh would be better off with Pablo's people and their primitive culture than with the devil who was his father. Curiously, the thought of Angel searching high and low for his son without success gave Rachel perverse pleasure.

The dangerous path curved with the face of the cliffs then dipped downward. They were starting their descent already. With her thoughts so preoccupied, she hadn't realized they had traveled so far. Rachel slowed as clouds once more concealed the moon. Sloan was behind her now. She didn't have to look, and she sure couldn't hear him, but he was there. She could feel him, just like always. She shivered with awareness. He moved with a stealth that was more animal like than human. The image of his muscular body moving over hers suddenly filled her mind. She shook her head to shatter the unbidden fantasy.

The feelings he elicited confused her—fear and desire; trust and danger. How could she desire a man she feared so completely? She couldn't understand it. She trusted him, yet she knew from his words and the intensity in those piercing blue eyes that he personified danger. Her feelings softened at the memory of how he had held Josh in his arms tonight. And Josh had let him, even snuggled close to Sloan's massive chest.

Holding her son that way was surely painful for Sloan. He had likely relived holding his own son in such a manner. But he hadn't complained. Sloan suffered in silence. She remembered the story Victoria Colby had told her. How could any man, no matter how strong, survive such a devastating loss? But Sloan had. He drank too much, put himself in harm's way every chance he got, but he survived. God surely had good things in store for a man who had suffered so very much and managed to survive day after day when a lesser man would have given up long ago. Sloan was a man of infinite courage.

Rachel considered Sloan's usual indifference toward her and life in general, then his hot kisses. He tried so hard not to care, but like her, he couldn't help himself. Not even where she was concerned. And he hated that fault, she realized with sudden clarity. He didn't want to feel anything for her, and she could scarcely blame him. She had slept with the enemy. She shuddered at the memory of Angel's touch. What a fool she had been. And yet, Sloan took her and Josh in, protected them. She had no doubt that he would give his own life to protect either of them. She hoped someday she would understand what made a man like Sloan give so very much for so little. He'd already given more than most.

Rachel hugged her arms around her middle. Could she do one thing for Sloan in repayment for all that he did for her and Josh? Sure she would pay his fee. Of course she had to nail him down to an amount before she could even do that. But that wasn't enough. She shook her head. Not nearly enough. Could she somehow show him that it was safe to trust his feelings again? That life wasn't only for those who had never been touched by the evil that had ripped his life apart? He deserved so much…she had to find a way to make him see that.

She would try. The decision made her almost giddy. If she could manage that one thing during the time she had left with Sloan, she would feel some sense of accomplishment. He needed to trust his heart again, to allow himself to feel. Rachel would give him that if it was within her power.

Distracted with her thoughts, her right foot slipped

on the loose rocks. She lost her balance. Ice slid through her veins as she struggled to stay vertical. Her bottom hit the ground hard, her full body weight thrown into the downward momentum now. She slid precariously close to the ledge. Rachel grabbed at anything in her reach to slow her slide. There was nothing to hang on to. She twisted her body, clawed at the rocky earth beneath her.

Her legs went over the edge. Fear paralyzed her throat. Her fingers locked around something...a limb or protruding root. *Dangling.* Her body dangled in the air. She refused to look down, though she was certain she could see nothing anyway. Sloan was calling her name, but she couldn't look up either. She couldn't move. All she could do was hang on to the limb that somehow protruded from the cliff.

"Dammit, Rachel, look at me."

She was going to die. A laugh bubbled up in her tightly constricted throat. Fate apparently planned to save Angel the trouble of killing her. *Josh.* He would miss her so much. He'd never had anyone but her...this would be so hard for him.

A strong hand suddenly gripped her right forearm. Rachel frowned and stared at the wide hand. *Sloan.* What was he doing? Her brow pleated in worry. He needed to stay back, he was only going to make her situation worse. Or get hurt himself.

"If you want to live you're going to have to help me out here," he growled, jerking Rachel from her haze of shock.

"I...I can't," she stammered. Terror washed through her again. Her hold on the limb slipped. She grasped it more tightly. Her palms were sweating. Damn. "I can't move."

He pulled on her arm. Rachel shrieked. "You're going to make me fall!"

"Damn it, you're going to fall anyway. Now grab on to my arm!"

Rachel gulped a ragged breath. She commanded her left hand to release its death grip on the limb and reach for Sloan. Her arm trembling, she reached for him. Her right hand shook with the added effort of holding on, supporting her full weight. She latched onto Sloan's shirtsleeve.

"I'm going to haul you up." His voice was strained. "But you're going to have to turn loose of the limb you're holding first."

The blood rushing through her body drowned out all sound but his voice. *Turn loose of the limb,* he had said. He wanted her to let go. But what if she fell? Or pulled him over the edge? The clouds parted, allowing the moon to spotlight her precarious situation. Her gaze connected with his fierce blue one. Her brain acknowledged the promise in those eyes.

"You have to trust me, Rachel," he urged.

"Don't drop me," she cried with his same urgency.

"Never."

Her body trembling, Rachel focused on the powerful hand gripping her forearm. She had to trust him or she was going to die. He wouldn't let her fall. Her eyes met his again and understanding passed between them. Rachel released the limb. Her weight sagged in Sloan's hold. Then he was pulling her upward. Over the ledge. Into his arms as he sat back on the ground.

"You scared the hell out of me." His hands were moving over her body. Checking for injury, assuring himself that she was unharmed.

Rachel slumped in his arms. She felt weak with relief. Her arms felt like overcooked noodles. She had almost fallen to her death, but Sloan had saved her. Now, as she sat safe in his arms, the pain of leaving Josh enshrouded her once more. She wanted to cry.

"You're okay now," he murmured near her cheek. The firm, warmth of his mouth caressed her skin.

Rachel didn't want to move. But he was lifting her. She wanted to close her eyes and forget this whole night.

"We have to hurry," he soothed as if feeling the need to explain why he couldn't keep holding her that way.

Somehow she was on her feet, his right arm around her waist, supporting her. She leaned against him and wrapped her arms around his lean waist. After all she had been through tonight she needed that simple pleasure.

RACHEL COULDN'T BE sure how much time passed, but she felt the change in the terrain beneath her feet. They had descended the mountain and were back on level ground, she decided. At least as level as the sandy earth and occasional clump of desert scrub got around here.

The wind whipped angrily against them, making their forward progress slow. Rachel huddled close to Sloan's big body for protection. They were walking directly into the wind, its force making each step a challenge now. Surely it wasn't far to the house. Rachel had no idea how far they had traveled or for how long.

"Wait."

Rachel looked up at Sloan, his face lost in the darkness created by the thickening clouds. He withdrew something from his pocket. A handkerchief. He folded it into a triangle and tied it around her mouth and nose.

Before she could ask why, the wind slashed them, sand stung her eyes.

"Keep your head down," he shouted above nature's fury.

She lowered her head and pressed closer to his body as they started forward again. He shielded her as best he could from the angry wind and blinding sand. His body was warm and inviting. He felt hard and amazingly male. Despite everything, her own body responded to his. The warmth and protection he offered had been sorely lacking in her life for so very long that Rachel couldn't help but want it when she finally found it.

What felt like hours later, but was probably only minutes, they reached the gate. Sloan entered the code and the huge iron bars opened. They stumbled through it and moved toward the house. The gate closed behind them with a teeth-rattling clang. The wind roared like a ferocious beast. Rachel shivered, thankful they were nearing the safety of the house.

Once they were inside Sloan ushered her to her room. "Get out of those clothes and get in the shower. Rinse your eyes," he ordered.

His tawny hair was tousled and sand clung to his skin wherever it was bare. His eyes were red. He had told her to keep her head down, but he'd had to watch where they were going.

"You need something for your eyes." A doctor was her first thought. The sand could damage his eyes permanently. She touched his cheek. "Is there a doctor we can call?"

He backed away from her touch. "I have eye drops." He nodded toward the bathroom door. "Take a shower."

He turned away before she could answer and strode out the door. Exhaustion weighed down on her then. Every step she had taken crossing that mountain manifested itself in her trembling limbs. Determined to follow his orders before she collapsed, Rachel trudged to the bathroom and turned on the shower. While the water heated she stripped off her sandy clothes. She caught a glimpse of herself in the mirror and grimaced. Though her eyes weren't as red as Sloan's, she looked a fright. She blinked, noticing the gritty feel for the first time. Her hair was a mess. Sand added new texture to her scalp and skin.

She stepped into the shower and allowed the warm water to work its magic. She had a feeling it would take plenty of soap and shampoo to wash away the layer of grit. But nothing would erase the dizzying emotions whirling inside her. Leaving Josh behind. Touching Sloan. Needing his touch.

She sagged against the tiled wall. She was hopeless.

SLOAN TOWEL-DRIED his body. Pain radiated through his right shoulder and he grimaced. He twisted at the waist to see in the mirror what he'd done to himself. It wasn't that bad. Just a scrape. He'd live. He tugged on clean jeans, but didn't bother to fully fasten them. Instead, he reached for the drops that would hopefully provide some relief for the fire in his eyes. He tilted his head back and dispensed two drops in each eye. His eyes squeezed shut, he waited for the medicine to do its job and for the new kind of burn to subside.

He tossed the drops on the counter and blinked to adjust his blurred vision. He threaded his fingers through his hair, pushing the damp mass away from his face. Muttering a curse, he flexed his right shoulder.

Though Rachel was a featherweight, pulling her up with one arm while holding on with the other had taken its toll. He slung the holstered weapon over his left shoulder. Angel or his watcher could show up anytime.

And this time Sloan would be ready.

Leaving the pile of sandy clothes on the bathroom floor, he padded barefoot into his bedroom. He needed a shirt, then he would check on Rachel. She'd gotten a little sand in her eyes, it wouldn't hurt for her to use the drops as well. The thought of her falling into that canyon still ignited fear inside him. The call had been too close for comfort. A soft knock jerked his gaze to the open doorway.

Looking uncertain and entirely too vulnerable, Rachel moistened her lips. To Sloan's irritation, his body responded instantly.

"I wanted to make sure you're okay," she said hesitantly.

He closed his eyes for a second and let go a weary breath. Maybe he had imagined her. When his eyes opened again, she was still there. What the hell was she concerned about him for? He didn't need her concern or anything else she had to offer. The arousal growing in his unfastened jeans defied his mental declaration.

"I'm fine." Sloan gave her his back and strode to the closet. He blocked the image of her standing in his doorway wearing only a T-shirt. Heat rushed through him at the memory of what lay beneath that thin cotton. Her pink nipples would bud at his slightest touch. He clenched his jaw and squashed the thought.

"You're hurt."

She was across the room and right behind him before

he could turn around. "It's nothing." He faced her, denying her access to his injured shoulder.

Her gaze narrowed in challenge. "If it's nothing, then let me see."

"I said—" he leaned intimidatingly nearer "—it's nothing."

"Liar," she retorted with a defiant lift of her chin. "I'm not leaving this room until you let me check it out."

Sloan breathed a four-letter word that made her eyes go wide. He abandoned the shirt he'd started to take from its hanger and turned his back to her.

"Damn." Her soft fingers traced the area near his right shoulder blade and down to his side beneath his arm. "This is a good deal more than nothing."

"It's just a scrape," he growled. Why the hell didn't she go to sleep? She had to be exhausted. The feel of her warm fingers was playing havoc with his ability to think clearly. "It'll heal without any help."

"Where's your first aid kit?" she insisted, ignoring his argument.

Slowly, deliberately, Sloan turned to face her. He glowered down at her, unable to completely mask the desire mushrooming inside him. His defense cracked when faced with the naive desire staring back at him from her big brown eyes. "Look," he began bluntly, "maybe you haven't noticed, but I'm as horny as hell. And you're only making things *harder.*"

The startled look that claimed her expression told him he had hit his mark. She visibly faltered. But his triumph was short lived when her gaze slid slowly down his body, paused at his half-open fly, then widened as a little hitch disrupted her breathing.

Sloan swore, another four-letter word that jerked her

gaze back up to his. "Go back to your room, Rachel, before you get more than you came in here for." Lust thickened his voice, but that couldn't be prevented. In about five seconds he was going to be beyond reasoning.

She danced back a step. Crimson bloomed on her cheeks. "The first aid kit," she mumbled. "If you'll just tell me where it is I'll get it."

He had to face the fact that she wasn't going to give up on playing doctor. Sloan heaved a disgusted breath. He supposed she felt some sort of compulsion to attend to his injury since he'd kept her from falling to her death.

"Fine." He planted his hands at his waist and allowed his gaze to travel slowly over her scantily clad body. "The first aid kit's in the kitchen under the sink." She turned to scurry away. "But—" she glanced back "—don't say I didn't warn you about keeping your distance."

She blinked, uncertain, then hurried from the room. Sloan shook his head. He was an idiot. He wanted her. He raked his fingers through his hair. He would have her if she set foot back in his bedroom tonight.

And tomorrow they would both regret it.

Chapter Nine

He had warned her.

Rachel hesitated outside Sloan's bedroom door. She shifted from one foot to the other, an attack of second thoughts throwing a damper on her enthusiasm. Gripping the first aid kit like a shield in both hands, she blew out a shaky breath. He meant what he said. She hadn't missed the fire in his eyes. A fire that burned for her. She chewed her lower lip. God help her, she wanted him, too.

She wasn't supposed to, she knew that. Sloan frightened her beyond reason on a level that had nothing to do with her physical safety, yet he drew her on so many other levels that she simply could not ignore the need. With each day that passed the desire to know him fully grew stronger.

She had to be crazy.

If she walked back into that room...this was insane. Rachel turned to go, but hesitated. The memory of the intensity in his eyes halted her. The promise that he would keep her safe when he reached for her as she hung on for her life, her legs dangling in thin air. The understanding in his eyes when she spoke of how Angel had seduced her...Sloan understood as no one else could. The pain in those same eyes each time he looked at Josh, but Sloan protected him just the same. Rachel had never known a man as selfless. She admired and respected him...as much as she had the only other man who had made her feel safe, her father.

But this man wanted the woman in her.

Just like she wanted the man in him.

If she never did anything else right in her entire life, she would do this. She knew deep in her heart that it was right. He needed her...much more so than even he knew. She understood that. The bitter indifference was nothing but a suit of armor he wore to protect his heart from further damage. Though Rachel was well aware that they had no future together, because of Josh...and what Angel had done, she could give Sloan the only thing she had to give. Her complete trust in the most intimate way a man and woman could come together. If that one act could make him feel again, could make him see that he could care, that he could give himself that way, then it would be worth it.

Rachel almost laughed at herself. What was she thinking? She was no savior. Hell, she had been too busy running for her life to even be a Good Samaritan these past five years. Besides, she reminded that part of her that wanted to reach out to him, Sloan had never once said he wanted to be saved. She drew in a deep, bolstering breath and released it slowly. But he did want her, physically anyway.

Before she totally lost her courage Rachel squared her shoulders and strode through the still open door. Across the room the French doors were open. Sloan stood, his back to her, staring out at the dark night. His long, tawny hair, still not completely dry, fell around his broad shoulders, curled around his nape. Her mouth parched as her gaze slid over that perfect butt she had admired on more than one occasion the past few days. She honestly could not recall ever having fixated on a man's butt. Not until Sloan.

He turned around and Rachel's heart leaped. His gaze skimmed her body, making her feel suddenly naked and entirely too warm. Electricity flowed beneath her skin when her own gaze moved over that beautifully sculpted torso. He took one step toward her. Just one, then waited.

Could he possibly feel a glimmer of the trepidation she felt right now?

"I found it." Rachel displayed the first aid kit like a prize. It was her acceptable excuse for entering his room again despite his warning. "It…it was right where you said it would be," she rushed on when he took another step.

His gaze never deviated from her. He simply watched while she mentally squirmed.

And she burned because of it. Burned for his touch, for the sound of his voice…

She gestured to one of the chairs flanking a table in the center of the room. "Sit down and I'll—" she blinked at the intensity now aimed directly into her eyes "—I'll tend that…nasty abrasion."

Unable to hold his gaze a moment longer she crossed to the table and opened the first aid kit. Its contents spilled across the shiny mahogany surface. Her cheeks flaming, she picked through the items as if contemplating the selection. At least this way she wouldn't have to look at him, and she would have something to do with her hands. He was closer now. Maybe this wasn't such a good idea after all. What did she know about reaching out to a man like Sloan?

He moved up behind her and Rachel could not prevent the shiver that raced up her spine. His wide hand closed over hers, stilling the fingers fishing through the scattered contents of the well-stocked kit. His thumb caressed her palm making her heart lurch.

"You're not afraid I'll make good on my warning." The fingers of his other hand threaded into her hair, then allowed the length of it to slip through them.

Rachel closed her eyes and savored the sensations that washed over her from his slightest touch. She shook her head in answer to his question. She was many things, unsure of her fate, unprepared for his impact to her heart, not certain of her ability to please him, but she was not afraid of him in that way. Not any more. Maybe she never was.

He released her hand only to wrap his arm around her waist and pull her close. The feel of his hard male body against her buttocks was almost more than she could bear. Her breath fled her lungs when he moved her hair aside to kiss her neck. Firm and hot, his lips teased her neck, made a path to her ear.

"Is this what you want?" He pressed her more firmly against his undeniable arousal.

Rachel couldn't contain the little sound that escaped her, half moan, half gasp.

He inhaled deeply against her hair, then hummed a note of pleasure. "You smell nice." His fingers splayed on her abdomen, pressing her closer still. His tongue traced the shell of her ear, she shivered. "But, I have to tell you," he rasped, then nipped her earlobe, "I've never been overly fond of virgins."

Rachel whipped around in his hold. She stared at him, stunned that he would say such a thing. "You know that's not true." Why was he doing this? Was he trying to push her away? Or simply playing some sort of game?

A wicked smile tilted one side of his full mouth, making her pulse skip. "I've read your file. I know everything there is to know. Not to mention that I undressed you."

Her cesarean section scar. She'd been in labor too long, Josh had gone into distress. But that didn't lend credit to his calling her a virgin.

"But Angel and I—"

His expression turned savage so fast that Rachel drew back from the fierceness of it. "I have my doubts as to whether he did the job right."

She shook her head, suddenly uneasy. Nothing he said made sense. "I don't understand."

He lowered his head, his gaze intent on hers. That fiery desire was back in his eyes again. "You will," he murmured before taking her mouth.

His kiss was greedy. He left no question as to what he wanted. The heat of it filled her so fast that she felt lightheaded. Her arms found their way around his neck. He lifted her against him and want arrowed straight to her feminine core. The feel of his chest against her breasts even through the thin cotton of her T-shirt made her weak with desire. His tongue slid over the seam of her lips, urging her to open for him. She opened instantly, unable to do otherwise. He thrust his tongue into her mouth and her thighs quivered. His hands moved beneath the hem of her T-shirt and squeezed her bottom, lifted her more firmly into him.

The groan that sounded could have come from either of them. Rachel didn't know nor did she care, she only wanted to feel more of him. Her fingers tunneled into his long hair, and she reveled in the silkiness of it. She had known it would feel like that. The rigid angle of his jaw, the corded length of his neck, then the smooth contours of his awesome chest. Her fingers learned them all. The taut ridges of his abdomen, his lean hips, the tight feel of his butt. Anticipation zipped through her, urging her seeking hands over his bare back, down his muscular sides. She wanted to touch him all over.

He ushered her into the chair behind her, then dropped to his knees between her thighs. His mouth left hers only long enough to drag the T-shirt over her head. Then he kissed her even harder, his tongue delving, touching, teasing, his hands circling her waist. He showered a trail of kisses down her throat, lingering at the pulse points, tasting her, making her crave more.

''Sloan,'' she whimpered.

His mouth closed over her breast and her inner muscles convulsed. She cried out, wanting to encourage him, but unsure how. The exquisite torture continued. He nibbled, licked, then suckled until she wanted to scream with the need building inside her. She wanted more, needed more, but more would only make the sweet agony last longer.

He worked the same magic on her other breast, while the long fingers of one hand plucked and kneaded the one he had abandoned. She plunged her fingers into his hair and urged him on. The feel of his tongue, his teeth, his lips against her sensitized nipple drove her mad. She wanted to touch him in the same way, but could not bring herself to put an end to the feel of his mouth on her.

His mouth moved to hers again, his hands cradled her face. He kissed her so thoroughly she wanted to weep. He stood, pulling her up as he went. He lifted her into his arms and carried her to his bed, his lips teasing her skin mercilessly as he lay her there.

With painstaking slowness, he dragged her panties down her legs, his palm skimming her flesh, making her burn for more of his touch. So many sensations whirled inside her, her body felt ready to explode. He moved from the bed and Rachel reached for him, her desperation palpable when confronted with the possible loss of his touch. He shed his jeans, then lowered his long frame next to hers. Her pulse quickened as her gaze roved the length of him. Rachel's whole body sighed at having him next to her again, but quickly burst into renewed flames at the look of need in his eyes.

His palm flattened on her abdomen, then slid lower until he cradled her intimately. Rachel's breath caught, but he pressed a soothing kiss to her parted lips. One long finger parted her feminine folds, teased her. She made a tiny, startled sound, he shushed her with his attentive lips. That same finger slipped inside her, making her quiver with a new rush of pleasure. Then another finger moved inside her, increasing the friction. She arched against his hand, her body aching for something she couldn't name. Her eyes closed with the need of it. He moved those two fingers rhythmically until she wanted to scream. Her body writhed uncontrollably. Her hips undulated beneath his assault. But it wasn't enough.

He stopped. Rachel clutched at him, needing him. She searched his face, her body burning to have him inside her, he only smiled as if he knew the secret and wasn't sure he intended to share it with her just yet.

"Please." She tugged him nearer. She had never

been on fire like this before. He had to do something before she lost her mind.

He covered her throbbing body with his own. His arousal pressed against her belly and for the first time Rachel felt a twinge of fear. She closed her eyes and arched upward, no longer caring, only needing. He moved between her thighs, which she spread in frantic invitation. His tip nudged her and she cried out his name.

He brushed a gentle kiss across her lips. "Open your eyes."

She obeyed and what she saw in his took her breath away. His need was every bit as desperate as hers. He took her hand and placed it on his heavy arousal. A surge of power rushed through her at the satiny feel of him. He was big and hard for her, because he wanted her. Her heart thudded, rushing her heated blood through her veins, fueling the desire vibrating her senses. With his help, she guided him to the part of her that ached to be filled by him.

He thrust his hips, entering her by slow, agonizing degrees. She couldn't breathe. She couldn't move. She could only stare into those searing blue eyes and take what he offered. The hot, stretching sensation sent waves of unexpected pleasure cascading over her like a waterfall. Those same muscles stretching to accommodate him, clenched tightly around him. Sloan groaned a savage sound. She had to close her eyes against the intensity of sensations she had never before experienced. Lights pulsed behind her lids. Her body tensed and wave after wave of pure sensation exploded around her. Somehow, in that state of elation just before she could take a breath, she realized that this was her climax.

And Sloan had been her first.

He thrust fully, filling her completely. Rachel gasped at the feel of him so deeply inside her. His ragged breath fanned her hungry lips as he stilled. He searched her face for a long moment, as if wanting to commit this moment to memory. He caressed her cheek with gentle fingers. He throbbed inside her, her own body already speeding toward the next peak she now recognized. The scent of their lovemaking filled her nostrils, warming her from the inside out. His skin felt hot where it melded with hers. She wanted to hold him forever, to make him feel what she was feeling right now.

She would have given her soul at that moment to read the indefinable emotion in his eyes. He shifted, burying himself deeper still, if that was possible. Just when she thought she would die if he looked at her that way one second longer, he lowered his mouth to hers. The kiss started out slow and tender, but quickly turned wild and frantic. He flexed his powerful hips. Rachel cried out, the sound lost to his kisses. Again and again, he thrust until release claimed her again, the rush even stronger this time. Then he came too. His groan of release loud and savage. He thrust one last time, filling her so completely that she knew precisely what he had meant earlier.

She had not been taken thoroughly by a man until tonight. And Sloan had been the one to take her fully. No man, not even Angel, had touched that place inside her.

Rachel closed her eyes so Sloan wouldn't see what she now knew. She had made a mistake. She had just given Sloan much more than she intended. And there was no way to take it back.

Her heart belonged to him.

Rachel was more than a little certain that he did not want her for more than what they had just shared, and he would certainly never want her heart.

He didn't even want his own.

SLOAN STOOD BENEATH the spray of hot water, his head pressed against the moist, tile wall, the water sluicing over his back. What had he done? He clutched at the slick walls and fought the pain knotting inside him. He was a fool. The act he and Rachel had just shared was not sex, and he knew it. He'd had sex plenty of times over the years. Sex could be just as hot, just as frantic, but sex brought physical satiation, not complete emotional turmoil.

They had made love.

He swore crudely. It was supposed to be about sex. He wasn't supposed to care. He damned sure wasn't supposed to feel like someone had taken a meat cleaver to his chest.

And he'd been right about her virginity. Angel, the sick bastard, might have tried to take it, but he'd failed. She had allowed Sloan inside—all the way inside. He breathed another curse between his clenched teeth. They had connected on some level that transcended the physical. He had known that kind of feeling only once before…

And look what it had cost him.

He was a damned bastard himself. He had taken everything she offered. He could have held back. He could have refused. But he hadn't.

He shut off the water with a violent twist. "Stupid bastard," he muttered as he stepped out of the shower. He had royally screwed up this time. Rachel Larson was as fragile as glass. Angel had seduced her, killed her father and plagued her life like a recurring nightmare. And what had he done? Taken her trust. She had reached out to him and he'd latched on with both hands, taking. Only taking.

Sloan swabbed at his body with a towel, too disgusted with himself to do the job right. He wanted to wash away the feel of her, the smell of her. He tossed the towel aside. A shaky breath sighed out of him as he stared at his reflection.

"So much for not getting involved," he muttered. "You're an idiot, Sloan."

He pulled on his pants, then his T-shirt. Well, he might be an idiot, but he wasn't stupid. Rachel Larson might think she cared about him—hell, she might even think that she loved him. But she couldn't, he assured himself once more. Not really. Whatever she might think she felt, he knew just how to diffuse any silly notions she might be harboring. All he needed was a couple of days and she would be back at square one. She would see the error of her ways and go back to believing him to be an even meaner bastard than she first thought.

Sunlight streamed into the bedroom by the time Sloan stalked out of the bathroom. Rachel slept trustingly in his bed. He swallowed tightly, refusing to relive even one moment of their lovemaking. And that's what it had been, no matter how he denied it. Her dark hair spilled across the white pillowcase, making him ache to run his fingers through it. Her creamy shoulders were bare, as was the rest of her sweet body beneath the sheet. He drew in a deep breath and released it slowly to fight the need rising inside him already.

Gritting his teeth against the response he knew

touching her would stir, he shook her none too gently. "Wake up, sleepyhead. We have work to do."

Her lids slowly fluttered open. She smiled, her face aglow with satiation. She stretched like a cat. "What time is it?" she asked sleepily.

He fixed her with the coldest look he could summon. "Time to work. You have twenty minutes." He turned away from the confusion that clouded her innocent face. He didn't need to see it to know he had just hurt her. Hell, he could feel it.

"Don't be late," he warned as he strode out of the room. He was a bastard all right. No better than the piece of crap who had raped her emotionally five years ago. Right now he had to focus on the confrontation with Angel. He couldn't afford the distraction Rachel represented. Just maybe if he kept her busy enough, exhausted enough and angry enough, she would keep her distance.

And he knew just how to do that.

"Hit it again, harder this time," Sloan commanded.

He watched as Rachel slammed her gloved fist into the punching bag once more.

"That's better. Now, back off and kick it like you mean it." He circled her position and watched her perform the little kickboxing routine he had taught her. "Not too shabby, for a girl."

She glared at him. Then kicked the bag like the move was intended for him.

Sloan winced dramatically, then resisted the urge to grin. Perfect, he thought. He wanted her pissed off. He wanted her to hate him. He might not be able to put the fear in her anymore, but he could sure as hell make her hate him.

Her damp T-shirt clung to her body, outlining those gorgeous little breasts. Sloan averted his gaze. He had worked her hard and his overbearing tactics seemed to be doing the trick if those drop-dead looks she kept directing his way were any indication. He had to rebuild that wall between them.

It was for her own good.

Not to mention his.

"Five more minutes," he told her. "Then do twenty laps in the pool and you can call it a day."

She stopped, midswing, and gaped at him. "Twenty laps! I've already done fifteen."

He quirked an eyebrow. "Twenty-five?"

She muttered a very unladylike curse. Sloan didn't even try to prevent his grin this time. She was too busy beating the hell out of the punching bag to notice anyway.

Whatever it takes, he reminded that part of him that wanted to take her in his arms and kiss the hell out of her. He set his jaw so hard his teeth were in danger of cracking. She was a client, nothing more. When this was over, she and her son would go back to their lives north of the border. Sloan had nothing to offer her.

And he...well, he would return to his usual existence. A few hours of passion couldn't change anything.

NEARLY AN HOUR later, her clothes tucked under one arm, a towel wrapped around her slender body, Rachel trudged across the courtyard after her laps. She looked beat. Sloan turned his attention back to the tequila in his glass. She couldn't have had more than two hours sleep this morning. And after the harrowing trip back from the village and having to leave Josh behind...

He caught himself. He would not feel any sympathy. No way. This course of action was best. He had to rebuild that mutual dislike that had first stood between them. Whatever it took to ensure she kept her distance.

"Hungry?" he asked as she neared. He propped his feet on the table and turned up his glass. The liquor's burn promised something he knew from recent experience it would not deliver—escape.

"No," she returned coldly. She paused only long enough to glare at him.

"Good." He deposited his empty glass on the table. "Cooking isn't one of my finer attributes. Maybe you could whip up something later," he suggested with a nonchalance that stiffened her spine. That last remark really ticked her off.

"Don't hold your breath," she snapped, then strode away, anger radiating from every beautiful inch of her.

The time moved at a snail's pace. He had no idea what time it was, he could only judge the passage of time by the empty bottle before him. And, as he suspected, it did nothing for him. Drinking had never kept him from performing well, on the job or in the sack, but it generally helped him not give a damn about much. He swore at his new run of bad luck. Hell, it didn't even do that anymore.

Sloan was reasonably sure whatever time it was, that Rachel had retired to her own room by now. With that in mind, he finally went inside.

The house was quiet. No television noise, no sweet feminine laughter. No pitter-patter of little feet. He forced the unbidden yearning away. Already he missed the kid's questions, his ceaseless energy. And Rachel's singsong voice as she played with her child. Her laughter whenever Josh did something funny. Dammit, this wasn't supposed to happen. He had sworn that no one would ever get this close to him again. And look at him. Brooding like he'd lost something that belonged to him.

When Sloan passed the great room something in his peripheral vision brought him up short. Rachel, asleep on the couch. He frowned. She was still wearing the damned wet swimsuit and towel. With a heavy breath he moved silently to the couch and sat down on the table in front of it. She was exhausted. Mentally and physically—and totally vulnerable to him.

And it was Sloan's fault.

He closed his eyes and tamped down the regret that rose inside him. He summoned the image of his wife and son and tried to remember how it felt to be with them. His son was no problem. He could feel the child in his arms, hear his voice. But he couldn't do the same with his wife. Each time he attempted to visualize some moment they had shared, Rachel invaded his senses. The feel of her hair slipping through his fingers, the taste of her lips, the smell of her skin.

Sloan shook off the desire already tightening his groin. He opened his eyes and watched her sleep as if that would help. Beneath all that beauty and vulnerability lay more determination than he had ever known in any woman. That combination of fire and fragility drew him when he wanted to push away. The courage it must have taken for her to come all this way to track down a stranger. And then to endure his treatment with hardly a fuss. How in the world had this woman and her son—Angel's son—crashed into his life and made such an unwanted impact?

"You're losing your touch, old man," he mumbled. Sloan settled his gaze on her pretty face. Maybe he was getting old, and soft...or plain stupid. Whatever the case, his was not the kind of business one could risk such lapses in judgment. He had to do something to speed things up before he made any more mistakes. They both needed this over.

He had his head on straight now. What happened last night would not happen again. He owed it to Rachel to save her from the real threat—him. Angel was no longer a threat to her or Josh.

Angel was a dead man.

He just didn't know it yet.

Chapter Ten

Rachel awoke to sunlight reaching across the room. She blinked to adjust to the brightness and then stared at the alarm clock on the bedside table. 9:00 a.m. Why hadn't Sloan come for her? They started at 6:00 a.m. every morning. She threw the cover back and sat up. Why had he allowed her to oversleep? She frowned at the thought that something might be wrong. He certainly hadn't mentioned foregoing the morning work-out when he roused her off the couch last night and forced her to eat the eggs he scrambled. Eggs and toast were his specialty, he had insisted. Rachel felt relatively certain that he had simply wanted to make sure she kept her strength up.

She pushed to her feet and padded to the bathroom. She had fallen asleep on the couch, wet swimsuit and all. The now dry garment hung across the shower door. And who wouldn't have fallen asleep? Sloan had pushed her harder than he ever had before. Had her supremely annoyed as a matter of fact. She still wanted to punch him instead of that damned bag.

She'd had hardly any sleep the night before with taking Josh to the village.

Josh.

Her heart squeezed at the thought of her little boy. She missed him so much. She blinked back the tears and forced herself to go through the motions of preparing for the day. Maybe that was the reason Sloan had kept her so busy yesterday. He had purposely made her angry with his little remarks and unnecessary physical torture. Her arms felt weak from all the laps in the pool. Giving him grace, he probably realized she needed the distraction and then the exhaustion of last night to keep her mind off her son.

And the lovemaking? Had she needed that too? She moistened her lips and swallowed at the dryness in her throat. Her body tingled even now at the thought of Sloan's lovemaking. She could not regret the act. It had touched her far too deeply. She had been right about Sloan. He had pleasured her to the point of madness before allowing himself the pleasure of release. He had been right as well. Though Angel had been her first sexual experience, he had not made love to her the way Sloan had. Not by a long shot.

Rachel closed her eyes and quaked with revulsion at the thought of Angel. There was no comparison between the men. Not in the intimate act she and Sloan had shared, nor in any other way. Angel was a selfish, greedy bastard who killed people for a living. She clenched her jaw against the outrage that instantly filled her at the thought of the man. He didn't just kill people, he relished in making an art of it. He stole into people's lives, then snatched that life away.

By contrast, Sloan was a good man. Despite the bitterness and indifference he radiated, worn as a shield about him, there was a good heart beating in that awesome chest. Even with the knowledge that Angel was Josh's father, Sloan still reached out to her son. Grudg-

ingly maybe, but he had done it just the same. He
would protect them with his life. There was no question
in Rachel's mind. Sloan would do whatever it took to
protect her and Josh. She closed her eyes and prayed
fervently that it wouldn't come down to that. Sloan
deserved to live and be happy again. Really happy.

But that happiness wouldn't be found with her. No
matter how sweetly and tenderly he had made love to
her, there was Josh. Even a good man would hesitate
about loving the son of the man who had murdered his
wife and child. This thing she felt for Sloan would
never work out. Rachel had to think about Josh. His
happiness was vastly more important than hers.

She made a mirthless sound and shook her head at
the confused woman in the mirror. What was she thinking? Sloan made love to her once and already she's
thinking about forever? *Get real, Rachel. The man
doesn't want forever with you or anyone else. He just
wants to be.* Disgusted with herself, she stamped back
into the bedroom and jerked a drawer open to find
something to wear. How could she be so naive? Sex,
that's all it had been to Sloan. She had to face that fact
and get on with it. How adolescent could she get? This
was no hot romance. Sex. She shivered. Great sex, but
nothing more.

A knock at the door made her jump. She pressed her
hand to her chest and let go a breath. This was ridiculous. Sloan would have warned her if there was any
immediate danger. The thought that Angel could show
up at any time streaked across her mind, and panic
detonated inside her once more.

"I hope you're up," came his gruff greeting.

She relaxed. "Come in." She held the jeans she had
pulled from her drawer against her chest as if the faded

cotton would provide some sort of protection against his too-seeing eyes. What was she so worried about? It wasn't as if he hadn't seen her already, and she was wearing a T-shirt.

The door swung open and Sloan filled the doorway, but didn't step into the room. Rachel breathed a sigh of relief. He hadn't burst into the room with news that Angel was here, and he didn't appear to want to come any closer. She wasn't sure she could handle an up-close encounter with him just yet. Her emotions were still too near the surface. The ever-present weapon strapped to his shoulder reminded her that anything could happen in the blink of an eye. Complacency was dangerous.

"Get dressed, we're going into town," he said curtly.

A frown tugged at her lips. "Why are we going into town?"

He shrugged one broad shoulder. "To do what most people do—to shop."

He couldn't be serious. "What?" She moved closer to get a better look at his eyes. The stubble that shadowed his jaw added to the ominous look radiating from those cold blue eyes. Iceman was back.

"Be ready in twenty minutes."

He turned to leave. "Have you lost your mind?" she demanded, effectively halting him.

The look he sent her way went right through her, cold, hard. "You have a problem with going into town?"

She flung her free arm heavenward, still clutching her jeans with the other. "Angel sent word two days ago that he was coming. You know he will. He could be here now, watching and waiting. Going to town isn't safe, it's insane!''

He studied her for a few seconds, his gaze considering. ''Angel's kills are always intimate. One on one, with no question as to why. Even if he is here, he won't make a move in public. He'll wait until he can make it personal.'' He paused, his gaze still searching hers. ''Do you trust me, Rachel?''

She blinked, taken aback. Her outrage deflated like a spent party balloon. Of course, she trusted him. That was the one thing she could be absolutely certain of. ''Yes.''

''Be ready in twenty minutes.''

She watched him walk away. Her chest tightened with the need to go after him, to touch him and hold him close. But he didn't want that, not from her, not now. All day yesterday he had acted as if their love-making had not happened. Obviously, it had not affected him as it had her. Rachel shook her head slowly from side to side. It was clear to her that she was more than simply inexperienced, she was completely without any relationship savvy at all. An emotional teenager trapped in a woman's body, with a child and who needed her to be a lot smarter than this.

Twenty minutes later, Rachel was ready. She had forgone her jeans and decided to wear her skirt and blouse. She hadn't worn the outfit since the day she arrived and it was her favorite. The long, silky skirt made her feel feminine. And it would be cooler than the jeans, she rationalized. She had braided her hair and dug around in her bag until she found her sunglasses. The eyewear would afford her some protection from Sloan's piercing gaze.

She went in search of Sloan before he could come

looking for her. No point in antagonizing him further. He was back to his old self again, and Rachel had learned the lesson that it was his way or no way.

"I'm ready," she announced upon finding him in the kitchen. "I hope I didn't keep you waiting."

"You usually do, so why change now?" He gestured to the coffeepot and shot her an unreadable look. "Coffee?"

Ignoring his terse remark, she shook her head to the offer of coffee, then followed him outside. He walked her to the passenger side of his Jeep and offered his hand in assistance.

"I think I can manage," she refused with a feigned smile.

"Suit yourself." He rounded the hood and settled behind the steering wheel before she could climb in and fasten her seat belt.

Careful not to let him catch her, Rachel studied Sloan's grim profile as he drove toward town. His own sunglasses shielded his eyes from her, but she could tell from the tightening of his jaw when to look away. Whenever Sloan decided to glance at her, his jaw tightened and the set of his mouth grew grimmer. Rachel sighed. She couldn't possibly hope to figure out what was going through his mind.

She stared out of the passing landscape and sadness engulfed her. She missed Josh so much. Her arms ached to hold him. She closed her eyes and allowed his image to envelop her. Was Pablo playing with him? Did he ask where his mommy was? Tears pooled in her eyes. Would this never be over so they could be together without worry?

"Don't think about it." Sloan's deep voice was gentle, soothing and totally unexpected.

Rachel opened her eyes, then blinked to hold back the tears. "I miss him."

His fingers tightened on the steering wheel, and she wondered if he wanted to reach out to her but restrained himself.

"He's safe. That's the important thing."

Sloan glanced at her, though she couldn't see his eyes she saw the change in the set of his rigid jaw. He had feelings for her, if nothing more than basic human compassion, which she had first thought him completely devoid of. Maybe their lovemaking had affected him to some extent.

"Think about something else," he suggested after turning his attention back to the road.

He was right. She had to think about something else or she would lose her mind. Josh was safe and that was the bottom line. Something Sloan had said to her that first day skittered into her fragmented thoughts.

"Were you serious when you said that you took your house from a drug lord?" The question sounded foolish, she realized, but she had to know the answer.

A hint of a smile played about his lips as he considered her question a moment before answering. "He owed me. When I collected he offered me anything he possessed as payment." A heart-stunning smile claimed those full lips then. "I told him I'd settle for the house. He agreed."

Disbelief widened her eyes. "What on earth did you do that would compel the man to give you his home?"

He shot her an assessing sideways glance from behind his sunglasses.

Maybe she didn't want to know.

"I brought his daughter home to him."

His voice had changed. Somber now.

"Where was she?" Rachel asked hesitantly.

The answer was long in coming, finally he spoke. "One of his competitors had kidnapped her. He planned to use her as leverage in a territorial dispute. When he was finished he would have killed her either way."

"How did you get her back?"

He cut her another of those quick looks. "I don't think you want to know."

Rachel shivered at the lethal quality in that simple statement. "So he gave you his house in return?"

"It wasn't that big a deal. He owns several others. He rarely stayed at this one."

"His daughter," Rachel began, "she wasn't harmed?"

"Not a hair on her pretty little head."

Another thought struck her. "This drug lord, surely he had men who worked for him that do…this sort of work."

"None he trusted with his daughter's life." Sloan slowed as they reached the edge of town. He looked at her again, she didn't have to see his eyes to know that he looked straight into hers. She felt him. "None as good as me."

If anyone can help you, Sloan can. She recalled Victoria Colby's words again. This was no ordinary man. She had known it the moment she laid eyes on him. She felt it in his every touch. And for all he gave in this life, fate had taken everything from him.

The harsh reality grieved her. She wanted to reach out to him, make him believe that it could be different. But nothing she could say or do would ever change the past…or reach his fiercely guarded heart.

By lunchtime Rachel had seen yet another side of

Sloan. All morning, he made a production of their shopping. He was more than simply attentive. He opened doors for her, touched her reassuringly at all the right times. Not once had she felt vulnerable under his watchful care. But what possessed him to bring her to town? To buy her clothes? And even toys for Josh. It didn't make sense. Especially considering yesterday's die-hard tactics.

The busy streets of Chihuahua teemed with excitement. Vendors peddling their wares, shoppers haggling in the marketplace. The open-air shops beckoned to passersby. Weavers and potters produced their goods right before her amazed eyes. The vibrancy and contrast excited Rachel. The city was colorful and noisy, and, quite frankly, exhilarating.

Or perhaps it was the man who led her through the streets who stole her breath. He held her hand, kept her close. Each time he whispered near her ear, desire sung through her veins. She used every possible excuse to touch him. Just looking at him in those body-hugging jeans and the open chambray shirt over a tight-fitting T-shirt made her tingle, made her want him. The bulge of his holstered weapon beneath his shirt made her feel secure in spite of the danger that might lurk nearby.

She had been right in her first impression of Sloan. He was more man than she had ever known, and he was dangerous.

A definite danger to her heart.

"One more stop before lunch okay with you?"

Rachel blinked away her worrisome thoughts and manufactured a smile. Sloan had tucked his sunglasses into his shirt pocket, those clear blue eyes analyzed her now, expectant and ever watchful.

"Sure, that's fine." *As long as I'm with you it doesn't matter,* she didn't add. God, she was pathetic.

He slid his arm around her waist and ushered her into a more modern shop. Shelves were chock-full of trinkets and assorted items she couldn't readily identify. There was hardly any room to walk around the abundance of merchandise stacked around the floor of the small shop.

"Wait here." Sloan left her near the door, but out of sight of those passing on the street.

Maybe he knew the owner, she considered, as he huddled at the counter with the heavyset man. The man glanced past Sloan's shoulder, smiling a secret smile. Rachel's forehead creased with curiosity. What was Sloan up to? Heaving a beleaguered sigh, she looked away. No point in trying to figure it out. If he wanted her to know, he would tell her.

A wrapped package under his left arm, Sloan rejoined her and hurried her through the door back onto the noisy street. He paused on the sidewalk, out of the path of the passing pedestrians and handed the package to her.

"This is for you." His eyes fairly sparkled with mischief, but his tone was oddly serious.

"But you've already bought too much for me and Josh," she protested.

"This is different." He gestured to the package. "Open it."

Resigned, Rachel tore the recycled brown paper from the rectangular object. What she found beneath the wrapping stunned her. A sketch pad and set of drawing pencils.

She lifted her gaze to his. "I don't know what to say." God, she didn't want to cry, but it seemed a definite possibility at the moment. No one since her father died had done anything this nice for her.

He shrugged. "Don't say anything. Draw something for me. A picture is worth a thousand words."

He wasn't nearly fast enough to mask the emotions in his gaze this time. Rachel saw the need there, saw the desire. He might try to pretend he was unaffected by her, but he wasn't. And now she knew for sure. Unable to stop herself, she threw her arms around his neck and hugged him, his unexpected gift clutched in her right hand.

"Thank you," she murmured. "This is the nicest thing anyone has ever done for me."

His arms tightened around her waist, holding her lower body firmly against his own, but he drew back slightly to peer down at her. "I'm glad you like it." Something sad flickered in his eyes, followed by a yearning that spoke to her more loudly than any words he could have said.

She couldn't say what possessed her at that moment, but all other thought flew from her head. She kissed him. She needed to kiss him. He needed to be kissed.

The noisy marketplace, the cars moving slowly by, the haggling of buyers and sellers all faded into insignificance. There was only Sloan and the way he was kissing her. His mouth moved tenderly over hers. His hands stoked the flames raging in her heated body. She tiptoed, wanting more of him, but he drew back. He looked as dazed as she felt, his ragged breath fanned her freshly kissed lips, kindling a new fire within her.

"Lunch," he reminded, the one word breathless with a raspy quality that oozed sexuality.

She nodded. "Lunch."

But food would never be enough to fill her hunger.

SLOAN KICKED A small stone, sending it skittering across the sand. He checked the weapon in his holster as he paused long enough to survey the rear gate and the lighted area that lay beyond it. Satisfied with what he found, he proceeded around the east end of the house, scanning the windows as he went. He knew the grounds were secure. Fernando, his export business never taken lightly, had spared no expense when installing his elaborate security system. No code, no entrance. Any movement within six feet of the wall tripped the alarm. You had to enter by a gate, and you could only do that with the code. If you attempted to climb over, the alarm tripped.

He entered the front door, then locked it and reset the alarm to night mode. Rachel had retired to her room with her prizes. He doubted he would see her again tonight. At least he hoped like hell he wouldn't see her again tonight.

He cursed himself all the way to the great room. He snagged his half-empty tequila bottle from the bar and didn't stop until he was outside on the patio. He didn't want to risk running into her if she decided she needed a drink of water, or simply wanted to say good-night. He kicked a chair from beneath the table and dropped into it.

Another curse hissed past his lips when he realized he had forgotten a glass. "Screw it," he muttered, then turned up the bottle for a long drink. When he came up for air, he sat the bottle on the table and closed his eyes. He propped his elbows on the table and massaged his aching temples.

He could kick himself if it would do any good. But it wouldn't, it was too frigging late. He had crossed the line and now Rachel would pay for his mistake. He swore and took another long pull from the bottle. It would have taken a blind man not to see the way she looked at him today. The foolish admiration and respect. And the other.

Dammit to hell. The woman was in love with him. He had screwed up royally. He was nothing now. A shell of a man. His life was bargain basement, all the best stuff was long gone. He was good at his job and nothing else. The only thing he had to offer her was Angel's head.

The woman deserved better than him. She was selling herself way too short. A muscle jerked in his jaw as he grabbed the bottle and turned it up once more. He swallowed long and hard. He scrubbed a hand over his face and leaned back in his chair. He had seduced her…or hell, maybe she had seduced him with her innocence. Whatever. He had known better. She didn't have enough experience to be wary of a man like him. He had warned her, but she came anyway. She just didn't realize what she was getting herself into.

He closed his eyes and tortured himself with the memories of making love to her. Her sweet responses. The taste of her skin. The feel of her snug body as she sheathed him. So damned tight. So hot. His loins grew heavy just thinking about being inside her. Her sweet lips tempted him beyond reason. Those big brown eyes, full of trust and vulnerability, made him ache to hold her. He had been furious with himself yesterday, his anger had protected him. Kept him from screwing up again. But watching her sleep last night had dissolved any rage he had tried desperately to hang on to.

He had tried to keep his prospective today. He had planned every step, careful to carry through with each. Whoever Angel had watching them had gotten an eyeful. Sloan was certain that Angel knew by now that the relationship between him and Rachel had gone beyond business. The son of a bitch would be seething. A smile tugged at Sloan's lips. He would move fast now.

The one thing Sloan had learned about Angel was to make the first move. He needed him off balance. Nothing got to Angel faster than someone moving in on his territory. Rachel and Josh were his, to Angel's way of thinking. The idea that Sloan now had them would be more than he could tolerate. He would be here soon. Very soon. And Sloan would be ready.

Sloan figured the woman who gave Josh the bear was Angel's watcher. She had either been with Angel long enough to know that little gift, and then the yellow ribbon, would send Sloan into a flashback or Angel had told her to give Josh that particular kind of bear. The tokens were meant to throw Sloan off balance. To remind him of what he had lost. It had worked, for a while anyway. But now he had the upper hand. Angel couldn't possibly know where Josh was. They had stolen across the mountain in the dead of night. The sandstorm had proved a blessing in disguise. It had blown away any tracks they left behind.

Josh was hidden safely away, and Sloan had Rachel. Angel would be irate. The bastard. Sloan took another long drink. The urge to kill the man was overwhelming. Then Rachel would be free. Free to raise Josh. To live her life. To marry and have more children.

For that reason Sloan would not touch her again. Even if she begged him, he would not touch her again. He hadn't meant for that one kiss today to turn so passionate. He had intended to stay in control. Too much was riding on this to make a mistake. He would not fail Rachel where Angel was concerned. And he would not allow this thing between them to go any further.

Rachel deserved a lifetime commitment and he had no life to offer. He stared at the bottle in his hand. Everything he was or dreamed of being died seven years ago. Even a woman as sweet and giving as Rachel couldn't resurrect the dead.

Chapter Eleven

A long hot soak in the tub had been just the ticket to relieve Rachel's aching muscles. Even with today's respite from Sloan's rigorous workout demands, the adventures of the last two days were tattooed onto every muscle of her body. Especially her feminine muscles. Her fingers stilled in their efforts to loosen her braided hair. Her heart quickened at the images that flashed before her eyes. Sloan's powerful body moving over hers, his skilled hands, the delicious torture of his equally skilled mouth.

She sighed. She shouldn't be feeling this way. Sloan didn't want her to want him, she knew that beyond a shadow of a doubt. He'd made that point crystal clear yesterday. Then today, he'd been more than a little reticent.

Except for that kiss. Heat shimmered through her at the memory. She had sneaked that one in on him. That stolen kiss. The beginnings of a smile teased her lips. He had held back at first, then he'd returned her kiss with the same fervor she felt. For just one fleeting instant afterward she had seen in his eyes what he wanted to hide, then it had been gone. Banished like the rest of the emotions he refused to feel.

He'd quickly reverted to the brooding man who confused and annoyed her so thoroughly. Rachel combed her fingers through her loosened hair. He didn't want this relationship. Why couldn't she get that concept through her thick skull? He didn't even want her, not really. He took what she offered, when she pushed the issue, but he didn't ask.

Exasperated, Rachel swore and stormed to her bedroom. Well, she couldn't help the way she felt. And she wasn't about to back off. She intended to show Sloan that it was okay to feel something, anything for another human being. Somehow she would make him see. He had lost so much, he should have a future with a woman who would appreciate the kind of man he was. A rush of jealousy zapped her. She didn't want another woman to make him happy. She wanted to do it herself.

"Optimistic fool," she muttered. She glared at the new dress and the art supplies he had bought for her. Why did he do that? Was it his way of trying to be nice? Payback for what he obviously considered as nothing more than a sexual favor? She stared down at the short, silk gown she wore. He had picked it out too. The way he'd caressed the fabric made her ache to feel his hands on her skin. Surely what they had shared touched him in some way. There had to be some reason why he spent the day so frivolously with her. The stuffed parrot and maracas he'd gotten for Josh waited on the dresser for his return. Josh would love them.

Rachel closed her eyes and resisted the urge to cry. She needed Josh back in her arms. She needed Pablo here to run interference. Then these out-of-control feelings would never have happened. She wouldn't have gotten caught up in this crazy need to make Sloan feel what he clearly did not want to.

Enough, she told herself. She'd started this, she would finish it. Sloan would not prevent her from reaching out to him. He didn't have to take what she offered, but she would offer just the same. She couldn't help herself. She cared too much to leave it this way. Her attempts, successful or not, might make all the difference. Decision made, she strode determinedly through the gigantic house looking for him. She would thank him again for his generosity and she would say good-night. It was the courteous thing to do. He might not care whether she was civil to him or not, but she did.

It didn't take her long to find him. An outside shower, open on three sides and designed for spraying off before or after swimming, had been built on the far end of the pool. Sloan stood beneath the spray of water, naked from the waist up. His shirt and holstered gun lay on a nearby bush. An almost empty tequila bottle hung from his right hand.

The water slid over his wet hair and down his chest to absorb into his already soaked jeans. While she watched he turned up the bottle and finished it off. He tossed it aside, it shattered where it fell. Rachel jerked at the sound. She moistened her lips and wondered if it would be wise to approach him in his present mood. She wasn't afraid of him, she reminded herself. He would never hurt her.

She moved closer, her eyes reveling in the way the wet jeans clung to his taut body. Her heart skipped a beat, then pounded in reaction. His broad shoulders and muscular chest drew her gaze upward. The water stopped and he pushed his hands over his face and hair, sweeping the wet length back. She thought of how few words he had spoken to her since that stolen kiss. Watching him now she recognized the thing most people missed when they looked at this fierce, almost hostile man, the pain. So very much pain.

He suffered in silence, with only the tequila for relief. It seemed impossible that such a strong and seemingly unfeeling man could be vulnerable to anything at all. But he definitely was. And somehow she intended to heal that deep hurt...just a little bit.

She moved closer still. His eyes opened as if he sensed her presence. Instinctively she knew he did. The pain in those clear blue depths made her breath catch, but he masked his feelings in an instant. The defiant set of his chin warned her not to waste her time.

"Are you all right?" she asked tentatively, venturing a step closer.

Ignoring her question, he banged his fist against the chrome control and the water showered over him once more. He shifted and lifted his face to the cold spray, and Rachel had no choice but to admire the perfect body displayed so enticingly in that wet denim. Lean, hard, and breath-stealingly male. When he turned back to her, his eyes still closed, she acknowledged the chiseled features of his face, and the blond stubble that glistened on his jaw. As handsome as sin, and every bit as seductive...and dangerous to her heart.

The water stopped and his eyes opened. His relaxed expression transformed into a glower with the realization that she hadn't left as he had silently ordered.

"What do you want?" The raspy growl skittered along her nerve endings.

"I...I wanted to say good night," she stammered, suddenly uncertain of herself beneath his fierce glare, "but then I found you like…like this and I was worried that maybe something was wrong."

"I'm just dandy," he said with a grimace. "Now go to bed." His gaze swept over her, and she didn't miss the glint of male hunger there.

Rachel crossed her arms over her chest. She should have worn something else. She was about as subtle as a sledgehammer between the eyes.

"I'm not going to bed," she informed him, defying his command, "until you tell me what's wrong. You've been acting strangely all afternoon." Though it was well past afternoon now, he knew what she meant.

He leaned against the shower wall and rubbed one wide palm over his tanned chest. "Coming out here dressed like that," he nodded at her slinky attire, "is risky business, Rachel." He made a speculative sound in his throat. "It makes a guy wonder if you're really worried about him or not. Maybe there's something else you're looking for."

Ire prickled her. "You bought it for me—didn't you want me to wear it?"

He held her gaze for two beats before looking away. "Yeah." He plowed his fingers through his wet hair. "I did."

Resisting the urge to run back inside the house and lock the door behind her, she walked straight up to him. He watched, gauging her intent.

"What's going on, Sloan? Yesterday you had nothing to say to me other than to order me around. Today suddenly you take me shopping." She shook her head. "I don't understand." She swallowed the lump of emotion rising in her throat. "We made love—" he flinched as if she'd slapped him, her heart sank, he didn't want to talk about it, but she went on anyway "—and suddenly we're back to barely speaking."

He leveled his unreadable gaze on hers for emphasis. "Today had nothing to do with…the sex."

She trembled with the anger mounting inside her. Sex. Was that all it was to him? Of course it was. She blinked twice, three times. She would not cry.

"Then what was today all about?" she demanded, erasing as much hurt as she could from her voice.

"Today was for Angel's benefit," he said bluntly, those emotionless eyes still fixed firmly on hers.

Dread pooled in her stomach, temporarily slowing her outrage. "What do you mean it was for Angel's benefit?"

He cocked his head belligerently. "What you want me to do, draw you a picture?"

Another surge of fury stiffened her spine. "I want you to answer the damned question."

"I wanted to make him jealous, so I escorted you around town like we were—" a humorless smile hitched up one corner of his mouth "—a couple. I'm sure his little friend couldn't get word to him fast enough."

He straightened, too close now. She held her ground in spite of the pulse-pounding adrenaline roaring through her. She would not back off. She needed to understand what he was getting at. Instinct warned that she wasn't going to like it.

He heaved a disinterested breath. "To Angel's way of thinking, you and the kid belong to him. So if I were you, I'd go back in the house and stay there, cause when he gets here he's gonna be pissed."

Rage more deadly than she had ever experienced before exploded inside her. None of the attention he had spared her was real. The gifts, the kisses, the lovemaking. It was all about revenge. Baiting the enemy. Drawing a line in the sand. She struggled to maintain her composure as she demanded calmly, "It was all about antagonizing Angel?" She knew the answer, but she wanted to hear him say the words. "Everything?" she pressed.

"Today was about Angel," he said flatly. "The sex was about giving you what you thought you wanted."

Tears welled in her eyes, betraying her. She wanted to rant at him. She was furious. She didn't want to cry. "I wasn't the only one who wanted it."

"I warned you to stay away." He captured a handful of her hair and allowed it to slip through his fingers. "What did you expect from a guy like me?"

One lone tear trickled past her hold. "I needed you," she said softly, her voice trembling.

Her words slammed into Sloan's middle like a sucker punch. This was the one thing he had wanted to avoid at all cost. Another tear rolled down her cheek, his gut clenched. He didn't want to hurt her. But she needed him to be something he just couldn't be, not for her, not for anyone.

"I told you in the beginning that I wasn't the man you think I am." *I'm nothing,* he didn't add. He shoved the damp hair back from his face. Dammit, why didn't she just go to bed and leave him be?

She moistened those full lips and lct go a heavy breath. "And I told you," she argued, then paused as another shudder trembled through her, "that you're the man I need."

His desire kindling already, there was no way to ignore the desperation filling those big brown eyes. He swore softly. "You don't need me," he repeated, his voice losing some of its conviction.

She shook her head in denial, then whispered, "More than you can know."

His need to hold her overrode his caution. He pulled her against him, his arms going around her as if it were the most natural thing in the world. She trembled in his hold. Sloan blocked any response to the hurt he knew would come next, but he couldn't let this happen.

He tipped her chin up so that he could look directly into her eyes. "What you need right now has nothing to do with me." Before she could protest, he shifted, pressing her back against the damp wall. He turned on the water. She gasped as the cool water sprinkled over her heated skin. The silk gown plastered to her skin, outlining her breasts, her thighs and that sweet place that lay between them. He devoured her with his eyes, every muscle in his body hardening so fast that his breath stalled in his chest. The spray of water stopped. He watched the rivulets slip down her bare skin, then disappear into the green silk.

Her nipples pebbled before his eyes. He licked his lips, restraining the urge to taste them. The only sound around them was that of their uneven breath, hers as ragged as his.

"Please," she urged, reaching for him, drawing him nearer. "I know you need me, too."

She lifted her mouth for him to take. He wanted her more than she could imagine. More than even he had dreamed possible. She had to understand that he couldn't be what she needed him to be. "That may be," he murmured, his lips so close to hers that he could feel their pull. Electricity fairly crackled between them. "But you don't need me."

He held her desire-clouded gaze in a kind of trance. He couldn't look away anymore than he could let her. He braced his right arm against the wall above her head, trapping her with his body in the same way he imprisoned her eyes with his own. A tiny hitch in her breathing signaled her approval. Determined to prove his point, he encircled her wrist with the fingers of his left hand and drew it up to her breast. She gasped when he placed her hand over the sensitive swell. He squeezed and kneaded using her fingers. She closed her eyes and shook her head, denying the pleasure.

"Look at me, Rachel." The softly uttered command was more guttural than he'd intended, but his own need was rushing toward desperation. "Look at me." He pinched her nipple between her thumb and forefinger, rolling the tight peak, then tugging the way he would do with his mouth.

Her lids fluttered open on a startled moan. "Stop," she insisted.

"Shh," he soothed. He would make her see if it killed him.

She strained toward his mouth, pleading for his possession. He squeezed her breast again, then moved to the other, kneading, squeezing. Her breath came faster. He struggled to slow his. It would be a miracle if he didn't come before she did. Her hips began to undulate, arching toward his aching arousal. He dragged her hand down her delicate rib cage to that part of her that pleaded for attention. Her eyes went wide when he pressed her hand firmly against her mound. She gasped. He stroked her harder. The fingers of her free hand found their way to his waistband and tugged. He placed those needy fingers on her breast and squeezed.

"No," she resisted, her eyes closing again in the pleasure she could no longer deny.

He stroked her harder, faster, knowing she was close now. She fought it, but he knew just how to make her surrender. She tensed, her body quivering. She cried out, the sound a combination of agony and ecstasy. His groin jerked in response.

Her eyes slowly opened, her breath coming in short pants. He peered down at her shuttered gaze. "See," he rasped, "you don't need me at all." Releasing her before he lost the last flimsy remnants of his control, he turned, snagged up his weapon and walked away. His whole body throbbed. Need ached savagely in his loins.

"Maybe you're right," she called after him, her voice still unsteady.

He hesitated, and turned around slowly to face her as he tugged the holster over his shoulder. The sight of her threatened his composure. Wet, her hair wild, her skin flushed from her recent climax, he wanted her like nothing or no one he had ever wanted before.

She lifted her chin and stared at him in magnificent defiance. She was gorgeous. "Maybe I don't need you," she agreed, her voice still husky. "But I want you." Her bare feet soundless on the tile, she moved toward him, a sensual vision in exotic green silk.

His pulse tripped. "Then you're a fool."

"Probably." She pushed the damp tendrils of hair from her cheek and met his gaze with steel in her own. "But I'm not a coward."

Uneasiness slid through him. "I see," he said with sudden clarity. "The big, brave protector you came all this way to find is really a coward. Is that it?" He squashed the little voice screaming for his attention.

He wasn't a coward. He wasn't afraid of anything, certainly not death.

"You're not brave," she said quietly. "You're hiding from the world." She flung her arms outward, her palms flared. "Look around you, Sloan," she ordered, her voice rising to match her anger. "Do you think these walls or your fancy security system is going to stop men like Angel?" She stabbed at his chest with her forefinger.

He flinched, not at her jab, but a delayed reaction to her words.

"Is all that bitterness and indifference you hide behind going to change the past?" She shook her head. "No. It won't bring your wife or your little boy back."

He swallowed, hard. Tears stung his eyes. "Just shut up," he said tightly. "You don't know what you're talking about."

"Losing your family wasn't enough," she continued, hammering at his defenses, "you had to lose yourself, too."

"You don't know anything about how I feel." Trembling inside, he turned away from her. He had to get out of here. He didn't want to hear this. He didn't want to feel any of this.

"You are a coward, Sloan."

He closed his eyes and struggled for control. The hurt, the need was almost more than he could bear. It swelled inside him, threatening to burst from him. She didn't understand. He couldn't take that chance again. Not ever again.

"You're afraid to take what you want—what you need—because you're afraid of losing again. So you pretend you don't care about anything or anyone. You *pretend,*" she added, driving the last nail in the coffin of his restraint, "that you don't care or want, but you do."

He turned around and closed the distance between them with slow, deliberate steps. When he was toe to toe with her, he stared into those wide velvety eyes for three long beats before he could speak at a normal decibel level. "You're sure you're willing to give what I want to take." His voice sounded strange to his own ears, thick with the desire simmering just beneath the surface, but at the same time deadly with the other raw emotions churning wildly.

"Yes."

His fingers plunged into her hair and pulled her mouth hard against his. Want exploded inside him. He had to have her. Now. He kissed her savagely until she gasped for breath. He lifted her then, and carried her straight to his bed, kicking the door closed behind him. He shrugged off his weapon and lowered it to the floor.

Unable to slow the building momentum, they tumbled onto the bed together, a tangle of arms and legs. Hands everywhere, their hungry mouths seeking, torturing. The sound of their ragged breathing shattering the silence. He couldn't wait. Couldn't stop the plunge toward completion. Her fingers wrenched his jeans open and tugged desperately at the wet denim. They groaned simultaneously, the sound reverberating in the kiss they could not bear to end. She pushed harder on the confining fabric. And suddenly he was free. Sloan jerked the damp silk above her thighs, pushed aside the scrap of lace and shoved into her in one long thrust. She screamed her pleasure. He shuddered with the release that crashed down on him the instant he entered her.

Her long legs wrapped around his, pulling him more deeply inside her. She kissed his chin, his lips. Her hands slid over his bare skin until she held him tightly in her arms.

He braced his weight on his elbows and stared into her eyes. Just looking into those huge brown eyes made him ache for the rest of what she offered. But that could never be. He would not take the risk. She smiled tentatively when he continued to stare so intently.

Sloan wanted to look away, but he couldn't. She cradled him so tightly that renewed need stirred in him already, or maybe it had never completely died. The sweetness of her lips tempted him even now, begged for his possession.

She traced the line of his jaw, her expression suddenly somber. "You mean a great deal to me, Sloan." She leveled her too serious gaze on his. "Nothing will ever change that. No matter what happens, I want you to know that. You're the bravest man I know."

He brushed his lips across hers. "So I'm not a coward after all?"

She blushed. "I was angry."

He hummed a sound of approval. "I like it when you put me in my place."

"I'm serious," she protested. "I just wanted you to know that I won't let you or anything else change my mind about how I feel."

"Is that a threat?" he teased.

"No," she huffed. "It's a promise."

It was his turn to be somber. "Be careful what you promise, Rachel." He flexed his hips. Her breath caught. Desire barbed low in his gut, urging him to thrust again. But he had to say what needed to be said first. She had to understand. "You might have second thoughts later. Things change." He trailed a finger down her smooth cheek. "Right now you've got me up on this pedestal, thinking I'm some sort of hero."

She squeezed his buttocks. "I don't want to talk." She wiggled her hips to punctuate her statement. Those wicked hands trailed up his sides, then smoothed over his chest, stopping only long enough to tweak his nipples. "I want to make up for lost time."

He groaned and grabbed her hands to pin them above her head. He nibbled at her mouth, retreating when she would have kissed him.

"Just remember," he murmured thickly. "I won't hold you to any promises you make tonight."

THE RINGING TELEPHONE woke him from the sweetest dream he'd ever had. The realization that Rachel was in bed with him, in his arms made his lips curl into a smile. He was dreaming of her. The phone rang again, disrupting his smile and his good mood. He glanced at the clock on the bedside table. 1:00 a.m. Who the hell would be calling at this time of night? Rachel snuggled closer to him. He watched her sleep a moment longer. So trusting, so giving.

Another insistent ring shattered the pleasant silence. Sloan swore and reached across the woman in his arms and snagged up the receiver.

"Yeah," he snapped.

The only sound he heard was a kind of mechanical hum that assured him someone was on the other end of the line but refused to speak.

"Who the hell is it?"

A strange scratchy sound.

Sloan clenched his jaw and prepared to hang up. The next sound he heard stopped him cold.

"Daddy…"

Mark.

"Daddy!" his son cried.

Chapter Twelve

"It wasn't a local call," he said quietly. "A cell phone probably."

Rachel stood a few feet away, watching the agony manifest itself in the lines and angles of his strong body. He'd pulled on a pair of jeans and a shirt, but hadn't bothered to button either. The holstered weapon hung loosely over his left shoulder. Pain and weariness etched itself across his handsome face. What could she do or say that would make that kind of suffering tolerable?

"You're sure it was him?" she asked hesitantly. She had awakened to Sloan standing naked next to the bed staring down at the telephone. She had never seen that much devastation in anyone's eyes. When she touched him, he'd trembled as if unable to bear even that slight human contact.

Sloan stared at the small, framed photograph he held in his hand. It was the first and only picture of his son Rachel had seen anywhere in the house. He'd had it tucked away in the right bottom drawer of his desk.

"It was his voice." He caressed the smiling face beneath the glass with his thumb. "It was the same recording Angel used seven years ago."

Rachel shuddered with the sudden, overwhelming urge to strangle Angel with her bare hands. How could he do this? Hadn't Sloan suffered enough? She shook her head slowly. He had agreed to help her and Josh, that decision had put him back in the line of fire.

"I made a mistake," he murmured.

Rachel wasn't sure if he was speaking to her or to the little boy with the curly blond hair and big blue eyes in the photograph. She only knew she had to reach out to him, to comfort him somehow. She moved closer and placed her hand on his arm.

"It wasn't your fault."

He stared at her hand for a moment, then turned his attention back to the child in the photograph. "I should have stopped." He exhaled a shaky breath. "But I didn't. I wanted to bring Angel down. To do what no one else had been able to do." He squeezed his eyes shut and rubbed his forehead with the tips of his fingers. But nothing was going to make those haunting memories go away. "That mistake cost me everything."

"You were only doing your job." Rachel slid her arms around his waist and held him. His arm went automatically around her shoulders, pulling her closer. Hope bloomed in her chest at that simple gesture.

"It was supposed to be between him and me." He closed his eyes against the horrifying images Rachel knew were replaying in his head. "I was following another lead on Angel late that night when I got the call." He fell silent for several long seconds. "I should have been at home with my family. Cops were everywhere when I got there. I pushed my way into the house and she...she was dead."

"I'm sorry." Rachel pressed her face against his

warm chest. Moisture spilled past her lashes. She didn't try to stop it, there was no point.

"The detective in charge wanted to know where our son was. He wasn't in the house. He wasn't at the neighbor's." Sloan swallowed hard. "He wasn't anywhere. Angel had taken him."

She felt him shudder, and she held him tighter.

"We searched for days, hoping we'd find him. Ran pictures of him in the newspaper and on the news. Somebody had to have seen something." His voice grew distant and lost all inflection. "No one came forward. Then the calls started. Every night." He laughed a mirthless sound. "At that point, I even prayed...but God wasn't listening. Or maybe I wasn't worthy of his ear." He exhaled a shaky breath. "For weeks we followed every lead, searched that damned city from top to bottom. While Angel continued to call and haunt me with my son's voice."

Rachel braced herself for what he would say next. The tension drained from his big body, leaving the hopelessness she knew had engulfed him seven years ago. She couldn't help imagining how she would feel if she lost Josh. She trembled beneath the immense anxiety of the mere thought.

"Two months, one week, and three days later we found his body," he continued. "For almost a year after that I searched for Angel," he said through gritted teeth. "I wanted him dead, but he'd vanished without a trace. I pushed harder and harder...until I lost it. And then there was nothing."

She swiped her eyes and struggled to keep her voice even. "Why is he doing this now? This is about my son, not yours."

"Payback for what I did today." Sloan placed the

precious photograph on his desk and turned to her. "We've got his attention now. You can bet he'll be here soon."

Rachel thanked God that Josh was hidden safely away. At the same time, she worried that Angel might kill her and Sloan, leaving Josh alone. No, she affirmed. That wasn't going to happen. Fate couldn't be that cruel again. But, if the worst did occur, Pablo would care for Josh. Rachel was certain of that. He would keep him hidden away until Angel stopped looking.

She leveled her gaze on Sloan's. "What do we do?"

He brushed her cheek with his knuckles. Concern flickered in his gaze. "You should get some sleep."

She shook her head adamantly. "How can I sleep knowing he may show up at any moment?"

"There's no way anyone is getting in here without me knowing it." He gifted her with a weary smile. "Trust me. I have a backup system for my backup system. He won't get in without setting off an alarm."

"I don't think I could sleep anyway." She shivered, suddenly cold wearing nothing but his shirt. "How about some coffee?"

Before Sloan could respond to her offer, a single chime sounded. His head went up. She recognized the tone as the warning that someone had opened an exterior door. "Stay right here," he ordered.

Fear gripped Rachel by the throat. She tunneled her fingers through her hair and tried to slow the pounding in her chest. She had to stay calm. Becoming hysterical would not help. She stood statue still as Sloan moved silently toward the door on the other side of the spacious office. He drew his weapon and paused before moving into the hall to listen. Pablo burst into the room, Josh in his arms.

"What's wrong?" Rachel flew to him, reaching for her child.

"Sorry, *señora,*" Pablo said breathlessly. "The fever started this afternoon. The healer could not bring it down. I had no choice but to bring him to you—"

"My God he's burning up." Rachel touched his cheeks, his forehead. A new kind of fear twisted inside her. She took Josh into her arms. His body was on fire. Hysteria climbed into her throat and lodged there. "We have to do something."

"Run a cold bath," Sloan instructed Pablo. "I'll get the ice."

Sloan disappeared before Rachel could gather her wits and comment.

"This way." Pablo ushered her into the hall.

Rachel followed him, Josh cradled in her arms, to their room. While Pablo ran the bath, Rachel stripped Josh down to his underwear. He whimpered but didn't rouse from the heavy sleep. There was no sign of any kind of injury. A virus? Something from the water or maybe the food? Was there a doctor in Florescitaf? What if he—? Rachel slammed the door on that line of thinking. She had to stay calm. She couldn't help Josh if she became hysterical.

Sloan came with the ice. Rachel carried Josh to the bathroom and watched as the two men readied the water. This couldn't be happening, she argued. But it was. Nausea burned the back of her throat, her knees felt suddenly weak.

"Let me have him." Sloan scooped Josh from her arms before she could react.

Rachel didn't want to let him go, but Sloan was already crouched in front of the tub with her son in his arms. She knelt beside him as he lowered Josh into the icy water. Her baby cried out. Rachel's heart squeezed painfully and a new rush of tears streamed down her cheeks.

"Shh, baby, it's okay," she soothed. His thin little body trembled and he sobbed softly. Rachel prayed like she had never prayed before. Sloan's words echoed inside her head. *I even prayed...but God wasn't listening.* God would listen tonight. He had to.

"Pablo," Sloan said over her head. "Take the Jeep into town and roust Doc Hernandez from his bed. Bring him back here with you if you have to do it at gunpoint. We can't risk leaving the house with the boy. Angel may be close by."

Pablo placed a hand on her shoulder and squeezed reassuringly. "He will be fine, *señora.* I will bring the doctor."

Rachel nodded, she couldn't speak. She could only watch her baby fight Sloan's efforts to keep his little body submerged. His feeble cries ripped her heart to shreds.

Five minutes or maybe fifteen passed, she couldn't say which, before Sloan jerked her from her near catatonic state by asking for towels. Rachel grabbed two from the cabinet and quickly wrapped them around her son as Sloan lifted him from the icy water.

"We need to get plenty of water down him," he told her as he carried Josh to the bed. "Do you have any Tylenol or anything like that for him?"

Her responses sluggish, Rachel nodded and tried to remember what she had done with her bag. The closet. She hurried to the closet and grabbed the bag and immediately uprighted it. She fished through the items until she found what she needed. With the chewable Tylenol in hand, she sat down on the side of the bed next to her baby. Sloan had pulled a sheet over him. The wet towels and underwear lay in a heap on the floor.

"I'll get a pitcher of water and a glass."

Rachel opened the small, plastic bottle and tapped out tiny, pink tablets. Her baby's drawn, pale face made her want to cry all over again. But she had to be strong for him. He would be upset if he saw her crying.

"Josh, sweetie, Mommy needs you to take your medicine." His dark eyes fluttered open and she held one tablet close to his chapped lips. He made no move to take it. "Please, baby, you have to chew it up and swallow it. It'll help you get better."

He opened his mouth and took the tablet. Rachel waited until she was sure he had chewed and swallowed it before she offered the next one. By the time the tablets were ingested, Sloan appeared with the water.

Rachel coaxed Josh into drinking as much of the water as possible before he fell into another heavy sleep. His temperature felt much lower now. Sloan produced a digital thermometer and according to it, his temp was only slightly above normal. Rachel breathed a tremendous sigh of relief. Now, if they could only keep it that way. But he would still need to see the doctor. She wanted to be sure he was all right.

Sloan smoothed a comforting hand over her hair. "Get some sleep, Rachel, I'll check on the two of you in a little while. If Josh's temperature starts to rise again, I'll wake you."

Too drained to respond verbally, Rachel nodded. She climbed into bed next to Josh and closed her eyes.

Sloan stayed in the room awhile before leaving. Though she was too exhausted to talk to him or even to open her eyes, she was glad he was there.

Just before she drifted off, she remembered to say another little prayer. This time to thank God for listening.

WHEN RACHEL WOKE again it was five in the morning. She smoothed her hand over Josh's face and was pleased to find his skin only slightly warmer than it should be. She sat up and reached for the medicine bottle on the night table. After tapping out more tablets, she roused Josh enough to chew and swallow them. She managed to get a few sips of water down him as well.

Reaching to the night table again, she pulled his favorite pajamas from the top drawer. He wouldn't like it if he woke up naked. He loved his pj's. After slipping the soft cotton outfit on him, she kissed his cheek.

Easing off the bed, she stretched her neck and shoulders. She must have slept in an awkward position. She should probably get dressed and find Sloan. She frowned when she considered that Pablo should be back by now. It wasn't that far to town. Surely the doctor hadn't come into the room and checked Josh without her realizing it. She was tired rightly enough, but not that tired.

She licked her lips and cringed at the bad taste in her mouth. Noticing the water still standing in the tub as she entered the bathroom, Rachel flipped the lever to drain it. Those frantic moments whirled in her head. Sloan had taken charge of Josh's care. Surely that meant something. He had to feel something for the child, no matter who his father was. Grimacing, she raked the brush through her tousled hair and scowled at the dark circles under her eyes. She looked a mess.

After washing up and brushing her teeth, she dressed in jeans and a T-shirt. She needed to talk to Sloan and see what the plan was for hiding Josh. Though she was thrilled to have him with her again, this new turn of events definitely required a new strategy. Josh was not safe here. Maybe not anywhere. Before leaving the room, she smiled down at her son and switched off the lamp on the bedside table.

Her stomach rumbled and Rachel suddenly remembered that she hadn't eaten dinner last night. Warmth glowed inside her when she considered what she had been doing. She hadn't been hungry earlier, by the time she decided she could eat she had been otherwise occupied. Sloan had attempted to prove that she didn't need him. Heat flushed her cheeks when she thought of the way he'd given her physical satisfaction without actually touching her himself. But he was wrong, it was his nearness, the sound of his voice that had pushed her over the edge. She closed her eyes and relived that moment when he filled her. She had thought she would surely die from the pleasure of it.

Rachel scolded herself for getting sidetracked. She checked on Josh once more then padded down the long hall in search of Sloan. She smiled when the scent of fresh-brewed coffee tickled her nose. She found him in the kitchen staring out the window at the lingering predawn darkness.

For one long moment she could only stand there and look at him. His arms crossed over his chest, one lean hip propped against the counter. Her body responded to him instantly, growing warm and moist. His hair was loose around his shoulders, the tawny length tempting her fingers. He turned to look at her and her pulse skipped when that mesmerizing blue gaze collided with hers.

The hint of a smile that touched his lips melted her bones. She was so in love with him. If she could spend the rest of her life right here with him, she would. All he would have to do is ask. But he wouldn't do that. Though she had seen with her own eyes the tender moments he shared with Josh, he could never love him the way she loved him. Josh was Angel's son, that was the cold hard fact. Rachel closed her eyes and turned away from what she knew would never truly be hers.

"Is Josh okay?"

Rachel jerked back to attention and produced a smile. She focused on his mouth, his hair, anything but his eyes. "Yes. His temp's still at a safe level."

"Good." He sounded distracted.

The frown that claimed his features snapped her gaze to his. "Is something wrong?" she asked.

He sighed as if contemplating whether to worry her with his concerns. "It's Pablo. He should have been back long before now. There's always the possibility that the Jeep broke down, but that's not likely. He would have walked back or into town. He has a sister there that he could have gone to for transportation."

Rachel stilled. The hunger she had felt only minutes ago fled. "You think something has happened to him?"

He leveled his gaze on hers. "I don't think it, I know it. The only thing that would keep Pablo from coming back is someone putting him out of commission."

No further explanation was required. He thought Pablo was dead. The realization hardened like a rock in her stomach. Despair swooped down and tore at her chest.

"What can we do?"

Resignation clouded his angular features. "Nothing, but wait."

Rachel suddenly needed to be with her son. "I think I'll…I'll check on Josh."

Angel was close.

She couldn't be sure why she abruptly sensed that reality. But she could feel it. Some instinct that erupted out of nowhere. She had to get to Josh. The urge consumed her. When another of those odd chimes sounded she wondered if Sloan had gone outside to look for Pablo or if maybe he had finally arrived with the doctor.

She stepped quietly into the bedroom, not wanting to wake her son. The French doors standing wide open captured her attention. Ice filled her veins. She flipped on the overhead light with numb fingers.

"Surprise, Mommy!"

Josh sat on the edge of the bed with a stranger. A woman. The long, dark-haired woman.

"It's the lady who gave me the bear from my daddy," he explained happily. He frowned then. "But I forgotted him in the mountains."

The woman stood, her moves catlike, and expertly leveled her weapon on Rachel. "I think we should step outside, don't you agree?"

Josh looked from one to the other, his face still flushed with his fever. "Mommy?" Uncertainty filled his little voice.

"It's okay, sweetie," she assured him.

"Unless, of course," the woman continued, "you'd like to settle this in here."

The woman was taller than Rachel, and thin. She looked every bit as menacing as Angel. Forcing herself to comply, Rachel started toward the French doors. "Outside is fine," she urged. She had to keep Josh out of the line of fire. Whoever this woman was, she might be crazy enough to do anything.

"Good thinking," the woman cooed saccharinely.

Rachel paused at the door and gave her son what might be his final smile from her. "Josh, you stay right here and Mommy'll be back soon."

He nodded hesitantly.

The woman shoved Rachel through the open doors and into the night air. "Move," she snapped.

"Who are you?"

She shoved Rachel again, toward the center of the courtyard. "Shut up."

"Did Angel send you?" Rachel demanded, trying not to show her fear. She prayed Josh would not wander outside when she didn't return quickly enough.

"Oh, he sent me all right," she sneered.

Rachel turned around, making the woman pull up short. "Where is he?" Her anger kicked up, chasing away just a little bit of the fear. She was going to die anyway. "Was he afraid to come himself?"

The woman laughed dryly. "I think you know better than that, little Miss Goody Two-shoes."

"Then why are you here?" If she was going to die, she at least had a right to know the reason.

"Don't you know? I came to kill you," the woman said tartly.

Rachel blinked. "Is that what Angel ordered you to do?"

"Not quite." She smirked. "I'm supposed to keep an eye on you, like always."

"Like always?" Rachel had never seen this woman before in her life.

"Whenever Angel is on an overseas assignment, I keep an eye on you and the kid."

So that's how he kept up with Rachel's business and attempts to elude him, besides using the bank transactions Sloan had pointed out. "Are you his partner?" she wanted to know.

She laughed again. "He doesn't have a partner, honey. I'm Tanya." She quirked a brow. "His lover."

"I don't understand." If Tanya was supposed to be watching their every move, why was she holding a gun on Rachel now? "Where is Angel?" Rachel insisted. "He's not man enough to do the job himself?"

She gave Rachel a knowing look. "You know as well as I do how much man he is," she said pointedly. "That's the problem."

Tanya wasn't just his lover, she was his *jealous* lover. She wanted Rachel out of the way. This was crazy. Please, Rachel prayed, help Sloan keep Josh safe.

"Angel will be here soon enough, but it'll be too late for you, I'm afraid. I'm sick of hearing about sweet little Rachel," Tanya said vehemently. "I want you out of the picture."

Rachel shook her head in disbelief. "He doesn't want me, he wants Josh." How could she think that Angel wanted *her?*

"He wants you all right," she argued, "in some sadistic way. He could've killed you long ago. I'm not risking that he'll pick you over me when it gets down to the nitty-gritty."

"Then he doesn't know you're here?" The big picture cleared in Rachel's head.

Tanya waved her weapon. "I told you, I'm supposed to keep an eye on you until he gets here. But when he gets here I'll just tell him that Sloan offed you, and that I took care of Sloan to save him the trouble."

"He won't believe that," Rachel countered, renewed fear rising inside her. "Why would Sloan want to kill me?"

"Revenge, of course," she said triumphantly. "Angel was seething after I told him about your little escapade in town yesterday morning. He even cut his time in Europe short. He's coming in this morning, rather than later in the afternoon. I won't have any trouble convincing him that Sloan went ballistic and killed you. And that he would have killed the kid if I hadn't intervened. He knows how close to the edge Sloan is."

Rachel realized then she had overlooked one important detail. "How did you get in here?"

She made a disparaging sound. "Pablo has a sister who lives in town. It was simple. He didn't want to watch her die a slow and painful death so he gave me the code to get inside."

"Where is he?" Fury swept over Rachel, vanquishing her fear. This woman was just as evil as Angel.

"Don't worry your pretty little head about that," she patronized. "Pablo's beyond anybody's help now."

"You're making a mistake," Rachel warned. How long would it take Sloan to realize she was no longer in the house? Would Josh go to him? "Angel will figure out what you did."

"He'll be too busy grieving," she said with obvious disgust. "And raising his son." She smiled, enjoying Rachel's visible distress.

Anxiety hurdling through her, Rachel went for

broke. "Why can't we come to some sort of mutually advantageous agreement?" There had to be some way to reach the woman.

Tanya rolled her eyes. "Don't be absurd. Why would I want to make a deal with you?"

"If you let me and Josh go, I swear we'll disappear and you'll never have to worry about us again." She mentally crossed her fingers. Surely the woman had a price. "I have money," she added quickly.

Tanya narrowed her gaze suspiciously. "I don't need your money. I have money." She shrugged. "Besides, Angel would only find you. You know that. You can't hide from him."

She knew that better than anyone. "Look, leave my son and Sloan out of it. Your problem is with me." The thought of Josh being taken by Angel and Sloan being hurt was more than Rachel could bear. She had already cost Pablo his life. She winced at the realization. "All you want is to get rid of me," she urged. "Leave Sloan and Josh out of this."

Tanya laughed. "Oh, this is rich. You're in love with the man. Did he tell you what Angel did to him?"

The phone call. "It was you," Rachel accused. "You played the tape."

"I'll bet that freaked out the poor bastard," she said proudly. "I thought the bear and the ribbon were pretty ingenious as well. The bear was an almost perfect match for the one his kid had."

"How could you do this?" Rachel searched the woman's face, her eyes, for some glimmer of goodness. Cold, calculating evil stared back at her.

"Easy. I had a good teacher. As soon as I discovered that you had come to Sloan, I rounded up Angel's bag of tricks designed specifically to trip this guy's trigger and followed you here.''

Rachel felt sick to her stomach. Tanya actually derived pleasure from torturing Sloan. Would this woman be raising her son when Angel was off doing what he did? The thought made Rachel faint with panic.

''Please,'' Rachel pleaded, ''there has to be a way to work this out.''

''No more talking.''

Tanya moved closer, she pressed the barrel of the weapon directly against Rachel's forehead. Rachel squeezed her eyes shut and braced herself for death.

''Time to send you where all good little girls go.''

Chapter Thirteen

"Drop it."

Sloan pressed the barrel of his Beretta a little harder into the back of the woman's head. Everything inside him stilled in anticipation of her next move.

"Be careful, Sloan," Angel's lover warned, "I'd hate to splatter her brains all over the place."

Dawn rushed across the desert, spilling its golden glow around them as the tense seconds turned to one minute, then two. Sloan turned off his fledgling emotions and adopted the no mercy attitude that had garnered his current hard-ass reputation.

"You have some reason to believe that she means something more to me than bait for Angel?"

Tanya stiffened. Uncertain. "I saw the two of you together. I *know* what she means to you."

Sloan eased closer in preparation of grabbing her by the throat. "You know what I showed you," he said softly, his voice lethal, purposely seductive.

She laughed a strained sound.

An unexpected weight slammed into Sloan's right leg, startling him. He jerked his gaze downward.

Josh.

Tanya picked that precise moment to act. She

whirled around, Rachel clutched like a shield in front
of her, the weapon pressed into her temple. Rachel's
eyes rounded in horror when her gaze lit on Josh. Sloan
swore silently and forced his attention on Tanya. He
couldn't allow Rachel or anything she was feeling to
distract him.

"Excellent," Tanya said with a sick smile in Josh's
direction. "Nothing like a little family reunion."

"Let her go." A dead calm settled over Sloan. He
took a bead right between Tanya's green eyes. His finger itched to pull the trigger.

"Back off, big boy, or she dies right in front of the
kid," she hissed through clenched teeth. "I came here
to do her, and I ain't leaving until it's done."

Josh clung more tightly to Sloan's leg. He could feel
the child's heart thudding in his chest. Sloan clenched
his jaw and took aim at Angel's whore.

"You'll die together then."

"No." Rachel held up her hand stop sign fashion.
"Get Josh out of here." She moistened her trembling
lips. "Please, Sloan, keep my baby safe. Just go."

Sloan squashed the emotions threatening to tear him
apart. He shook his head slowly from side to side. No
way in hell was he leaving her. "Not a chance."

"How touching."

The abrupt sound of the male voice made Sloan's
blood run cold.

Angel.

Sloan met that hellish black gaze. A flood of emotions hit him all at once, straining his hold on reality.
Rage, pain, vengeance vied for his attention.

"Angel," Tanya said nervously. She released her
death grip on Rachel. "I'm glad you're here. I was
just—"

"Save it." Angel's weapon was trained on Rachel, but his gaze was focused on Sloan. "Drop your weapon or I'll end it now," he warned Sloan.

Reluctant but certain that Rachel's life depended on his cooperation, Sloan lowered his weapon. His eyes never leaving Angel, he crouched and placed it on the ground.

Fury streaked across Angel's face as Sloan stood, unarmed. "I've been on a damn plane all night." He made a production of straightening his suit jacket, then smoothed a hand over the expensive fabric. "While you were here, playing house."

The best-dressed assassin in the world, Sloan suddenly remembered putting that in his report as he searched for Angel all those years ago. A lady's man. A frigging madman. Hatred twisted in Sloan's gut. Now was his chance. All he had to do was drop, snatch his weapon, roll and take his shot. He could kill Angel where he stood before he had a chance to react. But he couldn't risk Rachel's life. Or Josh's. A ragged breath shuddered through Sloan.

"Imagine my surprise," Angel said angrily, his attention diverting to Tanya, "when I arrived earlier than planned to find you," he glared at her briefly before shifting his wary gaze back to Sloan "poised to kill the mother of my child."

"You don't understand," Tanya argued, desperation rising in her voice.

"Big mistake." Angel shot her. Rachel gasped. Tanya staggered back, then crumpled to the ground knocking Rachel down as she went. Rachel shrieked and scrambled away from her. "Don't move," Angel ordered. Rachel froze.

In that moment of distraction, Sloan snatched up his

weapon and leveled it on Angel before he could regroup.

Angel smiled, acknowledging the smooth move. "Well. Looks like the proverbial Mexican standoff. How appropriate."

Sloan knew Angel was no fool. He kept his weapon trained on Rachel, knowing her life would mean a great deal more to Sloan than his own. The desire to kill the sick son of a bitch burst inside Sloan like shattering glass. He could taste the vengeance, the victory. His finger snugged around the trigger. The memory of his wife and his son rushed through him, weakening his restraint. The sound of Josh crying quietly, his little arms still tight around Sloan's leg invaded his senses, shoring up his resolve. He couldn't make a move with Josh in the line of fire, no matter how much he wanted to.

But the need to kill Angel pulled at him, like a powerful magnet. His body trembled with the effort of holding back the long awaited vengeance.

Angel's sinister smile widened. "Are you sure you want to do that?"

"Yes," Sloan rasped, his heart thundering in his ears. The desire was palpable, a physical ache.

Angel shrugged. "I only came here for my son." He flicked a disparaging glance at Rachel who hadn't moved a muscle. "I obviously can't trust her to keep him safe and away from losers like you." He leveled his confident black gaze on Sloan. "In fact, I'll sweeten the deal for you, old friend—"

"I'm not your friend," Sloan ground out, the urge to kill so strong now he couldn't draw in a decent breath. "I'm the man who's going to kill you if it's the last thing I ever do."

Angel laughed fearlessly. "No, I don't think so." He firmed his hold on the weapon aimed at Rachel. "It's quite clear to me that you've tasted what she has to offer, and I certainly have no use for her. It's ironic don't you think, that I've kept her from men all this time, and then you're the one to take her from me. But I'm a good sport. You keep the bitch, I'll take the boy, and we'll both be happy."

"Go to hell."

"Why don't you tell me what it's like there," Angel returned. "I'm quite certain that you're very familiar with the place."

"You're dead." Sloan braced himself for the recoil.

Angel sighed dramatically. "If you kill me then you'll never know what really happened to that sweet little boy of yours."

Sloan stiffened against the rage erupting inside him. "My son is dead."

Angel cocked his head and leveled a speculative gaze on him. "Are you certain of that?" He shrugged. "The body the police recovered could have been any child. After all, there wasn't much left to identify. I doubt DNA testing was even possible considering the condition of the…remains."

Sloan blinked back the remembered horror. He would not allow Angel to distract him with lies. "The teddy bear was my son's. And there were other details, other similarities."

"Well, now, that's true," Angel agreed. "But was the body your son's? It could have been one belonging to a child listed as a John Doe in a morgue in Los Angeles. The size and approximate age were right. But when a body is burned that badly, it's quite difficult to tell, don't you agree?"

Sloan trembled at the memory of demanding to see his child. The detective in charge of the investigation had warned him that it was pointless to put himself through it, but Sloan'd had to see for himself. There hadn't been any dental records. Mark had never been to the dentist. No way to really be sure.

"You know I'm right," Angel pressed. "You can't be sure."

Afraid to move for fear of causing some deadly chain reaction, Rachel stood absolutely still, watching the scene play out before her. Every fiber of her being longed to run to Josh, to protect him. But she couldn't risk even the slightest movement. Her heart ached for Sloan as she listened to the verbal torture inflicted by Angel. She wished she had a gun so she could kill the bastard herself. She glanced at Tanya's motionless form. Her weapon was still clutched in her right hand.

"It's simple really," Angel explained, drawing her attention back to the deadly standoff. "You let me walk out of here with my son and I'll give you the location of *your* son." Angel tapped his temple as if suddenly remembering something. "In fact, he celebrated his tenth birthday just last month."

Rachel's heart raced with anticipation. Could he be telling the truth? She staggered beneath the impact of what his words insinuated. He wanted to trade information about Sloan's son for Josh. Rachel's frantic gaze flew to Sloan. The difficulty of holding back from the vengeance his soul screamed for was outlined in his posture and every feature of his face. The rigid set of his jaw, the grim line of his lips.

"An even trade," Angel urged when Sloan remained silent. "Your son for mine."

The slightest hint of a new kind of fear trickled

through Rachel. No, she scolded mentally. Sloan would never do anything to harm Josh. Nothing could make him turn Josh over to Angel. She wouldn't believe that.

But what if Angel was telling the truth? What if Sloan's son was still alive? Would he trade her son for his own? Rachel looked at the man she loved with all her heart and she knew.

He would do the right thing.

Her breath caught as Sloan, his intent gaze never leaving Angel, reached down and pulled her son from behind him.

"He looks like you, you know," Angel badgered. "He even asks about his daddy from time to time," he added with a demented laugh.

A muscle flexed rhythmically in Sloan's rigid jaw. Angel had buried the knife deep in his chest, and then twisted. Rachel held her breath as the seconds ticked by before Sloan reacted. He pushed Josh in her direction. "Take him in the house," he ordered, the words raw, guttural.

"Don't move, Rachel," Angel warned. The slightest hint of desperation tinged his voice. "If you do, I will kill you. I should have done it a long time ago."

Rachel ushered Josh behind her. He clung to her as he had Sloan, burying his face against her hip in fear. She looked from Sloan to Angel. That satanic gaze latched onto hers and filled her with terror. He was on the edge now, poised to make a move. Adrenaline pumped through her veins, urging her to run, but at the same time nailing her to the spot.

"Go inside, Rachel," Sloan commanded, his fierce gaze reiterating the order. The savage sound of his words jerked her attention back to him. *"Now."*

But she couldn't leave him. From the corner of her

eye, she saw Angel's aim swing from her to Sloan. Sloan realized his mistake instantly. Rachel saw the recognition that he had just traded his life for hers flicker across his face, then the determination that he would take Angel with him.

A shot rang out, shattering the tension. The look of utter surprise on Angel's face prevented his instinctive reaction to return fire. He stared down in disbelief at the hole in his chest as he dropped to his knees. The pale gray shirt he wore swiftly turned crimson with his blood.

"If I can't have you," Tanya mumbled, "no one can." Satisfied when Angel collapsed facedown, she dropped her weapon and slumped back to the ground.

Josh cried out in fear. Rachel fell to her knees and grabbed him in her arms. She pressed his face against her chest and made soft shushing sounds to comfort him.

Sirens blared in the distance. The police? Rachel wondered vaguely. Had Sloan called them before coming outside? Sloan walked over to Angel and rolled him onto his back with one foot to be sure he was good and dead. Then he stepped over to Tanya, kicked her weapon away and knelt next to her. She made a sound, more groan than word.

"Don't try to talk," he told her, his voice still cold and emotionless. He shouldered out of his shirt and quickly wadded it. He pressed it firmly down over the wound in her chest to staunch the flow of blood.

Hot tears rolled down Rachel's cheeks as she watched Sloan do what he could to help Tanya, though she didn't deserve it. The sirens were closer now.

"Mommy, hold me," Josh cried, tugging at her blouse.

Rachel held him tighter. "I love you, sweetie," she whispered against his hair. "Everything's going to be okay." She inhaled deeply of his sweet scent and thanked God again that he had answered her prayers tonight.

She opened her eyes and blinked to clear them. Angel was dead. Relief washed over her, making her weak and giddy at the same time.

Angel was dead.

She and Josh were free.

THE MEDICAL ATTENDANTS loaded Tanya into the ambulance and left, their siren screeching urgently. Rachel had long since collapsed into a chair, Josh asleep in her arms. One police officer was still questioning Sloan. Rachel had already answered their questions as best she could. Between their poor English and her nonexistent Spanish, Sloan'd had to act as translator.

Another officer covered Angel's body. Rachel closed her eyes against the image of blood pooling around him. The police seemed satisfied with Sloan's explanation of what happened.

Thank God Pablo was not dead. The police had found him in the Jeep on the edge of town. He had very nearly bled to death from Tanya's single shot to his midsection. He had managed to tell the police what was about to go down at Sloan's residence before passing out from his injury.

Rachel frowned as she realized that she had not thanked Sloan. He had been prepared to die for her. Had saved her life as well as Josh's. She had to thank him. To tell him she loved him. The thought warmed her. She loved him so much, she could hardly hold back from shouting it to anyone who would listen.

She scanned the courtyard for the man who made her tremble with just a look, but didn't see him. Holding Josh against her chest, Rachel pushed to her feet and went in search of either Sloan or the one officer who spoke pretty decent English. Maybe they were in the house, she decided as she headed in that direction.

The officer she hoped to find stepped through the French doors just as Rachel started inside.

He nodded. "*Señora,* we will take the body now."

Rachel's stomach roiled. He was talking about Angel. She blew out a breath in hopes of slowing the churning in her stomach. "I understand."

She stepped aside as two men pulling a gurney hustled past. She wished she could dredge up at least a little remorse that a life had been lost today, but she couldn't. Angel deserved to die. She shivered, remembering the sound of his voice, his touch. The urge to gag was overwhelming.

"You must sit down," the officer suggested.

Rachel felt the color drain from her face. She was dangerously close to fainting. She shook her head, clearing it of the hideous memories.

"No, I'm okay," she insisted. "Where's Sloan?"

"The hospital," he explained. "To see his amigo."

He'd left without saying goodbye. Rachel couldn't stop the hurt that accompanied that actuality. The sound of the gurney's wheels rattling over the tile tugged Rachel from her worrisome thoughts. Her arms tightened around Josh and she pressed his head against her shoulder, protecting him as the loaded gurney passed, as if even in death Angel might reach out for him.

But Angel was dead.

And Sloan would never know for sure if his son was

alive or not. That comprehension shattered Rachel's newfound feeling of relief. In helping her, Sloan had faced his own personal nightmare all over again. Tears burned Rachel's eyes. A sob tore at her throat. God, it was true. Even in death, Angel reached out to haunt Sloan. He'd made sure of that. He'd left Sloan with a thread of hope that his son might still be alive somewhere. Sweet Jesus, how was he supposed to live with that?

The sob broke loose and Rachel clamped her hand over her mouth to hold back the next one. Her freedom had cost Sloan his. This new ray of hope would be like a prison around his heart, never allowing him to put the past behind him.

"*Señora,* you must say if there is something I can do," the kind officer urged gently.

Rachel sucked in a harsh breath and fought to hold onto some semblance of composure. "I need a ride to the hospital."

He nodded. "I am finished here. I will take you."

He led Rachel to his Jeep and held Josh while she climbed inside. Once Josh was settled on her lap she considered her plan. Angel was dead. He had taken the truth about Sloan's son with him, there was no changing that. However, Tanya was still alive, barely, but alive just the same.

Rachel prayed with all her heart that Tanya would know Angel's secret.

And that she would be willing to tell it to Rachel.

JOSH GIGGLED AS the young doctor tickled him. A smile crept across Rachel's mouth. Josh bore no visible aftereffects from this morning's ordeal. She was im-

mensely thankful for that. But later she would have him
checked out by a psychologist just the same.

"Your son is fine, *señora*," the doctor announced.

Rachel scooped Josh into her arms. "Thank you,
Doctor. I wanted to be sure that there was nothing to
worry about after that high fever."

"He is fine." The young man smiled at Josh. "Very
fine."

"Where would I find surgery?" She needed to check
on Tanya's condition.

The doctor pointed upward. "One floor up."

Rachel thanked him again, then wandered the halls
until she found the elevator. Once she found the nurses'
desk, the next hurdle would be communicating.

The second floor nurses' desk buzzed with activity.
Rachel approached cautiously, surveying the busy faces
for the one who looked the most sociable. The young-
est one, she decided.

"Excuse me," Rachel said hesitantly. "Do you
speak English?"

The young woman smiled. "Yes, may I help you?"
Her long dark hair was smoothed into a neat bun. Her
uniform was a crisp white against her olive skin.

"A woman, about thirty, was brought in a couple of
hours ago with a gunshot wound. Is she still in surgery?"

The nurse nodded toward a set of double doors at
the end of the long corridor. A policeman stood guard
nearby. "She is still in surgery."

Rachel moistened her lips, her heart pounding within
her rib cage. This was her only chance to help Sloan.
Tanya had to make it. "Do you have any idea how
she's doing?"

The nurse shook her head. "It will be many hours yet."

Rachel nodded, trying not to show her disappointment. "Thank you." Josh stirred restlessly in her arms. She turned to go, wondering what she should do now.

"If you would like to wait," the nurse suggested. "There is a small waiting room." She gestured to the other end of the floor. "I will let you know when your friend is in a room."

Rachel smiled and thanked her. She set Josh on his feet and led him to the room the nurse had indicated. She settled into one of the well-worn chairs, realizing for the first time how exhausted she was. She clasped her hands and rested her elbows on her knees. Rachel pressed her forehead to her hands and prayed once more that Tanya would survive. Though the woman was far from her friend, she was Rachel's only hope that Angel's secret had not gone with him to his grave.

Morning stretched into afternoon and Rachel grew restless. She and Josh had found the cafeteria and had lunch a couple of hours ago. She had worked up the nerve to stop by Pablo's room as well. Sloan wasn't there. Pablo had been sleeping, but his nurse had assured Rachel that he was doing well and would fully recover. She tried not to think about why Sloan had disappeared so suddenly.

Rachel paced the length of the small waiting room once more. Josh was engrossed in a cartoon where all the characters spoke Spanish. Though she knew he didn't understand a single world, he laughed at all the appropriate times. She supposed cartoon antics were a universal language.

"*Señora.*"

Rachel spun around at the sound of the young nurse's voice. "Yes."

"Your friend has left recovery and is in a room now," she said in broken English.

"Could you show me where?"

The nurse nodded. Rachel pulled a reluctant Josh into her arms and hurried after the nurse. Anticipation sped through her. Please let Tanya know about Sloan's son, she chanted. When they reached the room an officer was standing guard outside. Rachel eyed him with growing trepidation. What if he wouldn't let her see Tanya?

"Thank you," she told the nurse as she hastened back to her post.

The police officer eyed Rachel just as warily as she had him moments ago. "May I help you, *señora?*"

"Yes." She put Josh down. "Sweetie, I want you to sit down right here." She pointed to the floor next to the officer's chair. "And look at the book." He had carried one with him from the waiting room. Rachel would have to see that he replaced it before they left the hospital.

Josh settled on the floor and immediately began flipping through the pages. Rachel breathed a sigh of relief. He was still wearing his pajamas, and with no shoes. But there had been no time for thinking about clothes. She shook her head, then straightened to face the officer who stood between her and Tanya.

She took a calming breath and forced herself to speak slowly to ensure he understood. "I'm sorry but I don't speak Spanish."

"I speak English well," he assured her.

Rachel nodded her appreciation. "It's very, very important that I speak to the lady in the room."

He looked doubtful. "I am not sure that is a good idea, *señora*. This woman is a murder suspect."

"I know. But it's very important. You can leave the door open or you can come inside with me. I just have to ask her a couple of questions." Rachel aimed her most persuasive gaze at the young officer. "It's very important."

He shifted nervously. "All right," he finally relented. "But only for one moment. The door must be open."

"Thank you." She glanced at Josh.

"The boy can stay with me." The officer pushed the door open and stepped aside.

Rachel smiled, barely containing her tears of gratitude. The room was quiet except for the beeping monitor at Tanya's bedside. Everything was white from the walls to the floors. Tanya's long dark hair looked stark against the white sheets. She was pale. Two IVs hung above her head.

Tanya's eyes opened as Rachel paused near her bedside.

"What do you want?" she asked in a voice rusty with thirst.

"Would you like a drink?" Rachel offered.

Tanya nodded once. Rachel poured water from the pitcher into the cup. She removed the wrapper from a straw and placed it in the cup of water. She held the straw to Tanya's lips so that she could wet her dry throat.

Tanya stared up at her then, suspicion cluttering her expression. "What do you want?"

What if she wouldn't tell her the truth? What if she didn't know? "How long have you been with Angel?" she finally asked.

She barked a humorless laugh. "What do you care?"

"Please." Rachel grasped the bed rail. "It's important."

She huffed a disgusted breath. "Ten years, probably the same amount of time I'll do in prison for killing the bastard."

"Then you know about Sloan's son," Rachel suggested carefully.

"If you're expecting me to admit I had something to do with anything Angel has done, forget it." She swore hotly. "I ain't taking the rap for nothing he did."

"No, it's not that," Rachel explained quickly. "I need to know if you can tell me what really happened to the child."

Tanya smirked. "Damn, you've got it bad."

"Please." Rachel held her breath as she waited for her to answer.

"Well, I guess Sloan probably did save my life. I owe him that much." She fixed her gaze on Rachel's. "Listen up, 'cause I'm only going to admit this once."

Rachel leaned closer to hear the words about to be spoken for her ears only.

"He was going to kill the kid once he'd finished toying with Sloan."

Rachel's heart quivered in her chest.

"But Katrina, Angel's only sibling, begged him to let her have the kid. She couldn't have kids of her own. Some kind of disease. Anyway, Angel finally agreed."

Rachel's breath evaporated in her lungs. "So Sloan's son is alive." The words were a mere whisper...a thought spoken.

"Yeah. He lives with Katrina in Detroit."

"You have the address?"

Tanya breathed an exasperated breath.

"And you're sure," Rachel pressed. "You're sure the boy is Sloan's son?"

"I'm positive. Sloan's son is *alive*."

Chapter Fourteen

"Mrs. Colby?"

"Yes."

Rachel clutched the pay phone's receiver to her ear. "This is Rachel Larson. Angel is dead."

A long moment of silence filled the staticky line. "And Sloan?"

"He's fine." *I think,* Rachel didn't add. She summoned her courage and forged ahead. "Does that offer to help still stand?"

"Of course," Victoria said without hesitation. "What do you need?"

Rachel held tightly to Josh's hand as she said the words aloud to another human being. "There's a strong possibility that Sloan's son is alive."

Another long silence echoed across the line. "How can that be? What about the body?"

"According to Angel's longtime girlfriend, he stole a body from a morgue in L.A. He set it up to look like Sloan's son, even made sure there would be no way to identify it."

"Why would he go to all that trouble?" Victoria asked, still suspect.

Rachel quickly explained about Angel's sister, and where she lived now according to Tanya.

"It'll take a couple of days to check it out, but I'll put Ric Martinez right on it."

"Thank you."

"Don't thank me," Victoria said quietly. "If there's any chance that Sloan's son is alive, I'll do whatever it takes to find him. I'll send Zach Ashton along as well. He's our top legal advisor."

Rachel ended the call and decided she had one more stop before leaving the hospital.

Pablo was watching television when Rachel and Josh entered his room. A woman sat next to his bed.

"Señora Rachel, Josh! It is good to see you."

Rachel lifted Josh up so he could shake hands with Pablo. Rachel kissed the man's cheek in lieu of a handshake. Pablo blushed and patted her hand.

"This is my sister, Rosa."

"It's very nice to meet you, Rosa." Rachel beamed a smile at her. The resemblance between Rosa and her brother was easy to see. Same thin features. Same gentle smile.

The woman nodded and said something in Spanish.

"She's not much for the English," he explained.

Rachel shrugged. "That's okay. I'm not much for the Spanish." She placed her hand on his and squeezed affectionately. "You're doing okay?"

"Very fine. Yes." His gaze turned somber. "I'm glad the evil man is dead."

Rachel sighed. "Me, too."

"The woman who shot me, she is here in the hospital?"

"Yes, but she's under guard. She won't be going anywhere except to prison when she is well enough."

Pablo nodded. "Good."

"I haven't seen Sloan since I left the house." Rachel ventured.

"He had urgent business." Pablo took her hand in his this time. "Give him time."

"He left without saying anything, even goodbye," Rachel told him, unable to hide her hurt. "I'm sure he knows I've been at the hospital today, but he's avoided me. I don't understand."

"Don't doubt his heart, *señora*," Pablo insisted. "But you must give him time. He is afraid to admit his feelings. He has lost so much in his life. It is difficult to risk such great pain again."

Rachel wished she could tell Pablo that Sloan's son might be alive, but she had to be sure first. It would be too painful to get Sloan's hopes up, and Pablo would surely tell Sloan about the investigation.

"I'm taking a room in the hotel across the street."

Pablo nodded. "I know the one."

"Would you please tell Sloan that if he wants to see me I'll be waiting there."

"Yes, I'll tell him. He will be back day after tomorrow."

Rachel hesitated before turning away. "Did he say or ask anything at all about me when he was here earlier?"

Pablo stared at his hands. "I'm sorry, Señora Rachel, but he did not. He was called away very suddenly."

"Well." Rachel blinked back the tears of disappointment. How convenient that he was called away so suddenly. She forced the bitter hurt away. "I should be going." She kissed Pablo's forehead, making him blush again, then smiled for Rosa. She had to get out of here. She needed time away from everyone to grieve for what she had hoped could be, but never would. Later, when Josh was fast asleep, Rachel would allow the soul-shaking tears to fall, but not now.

TWO OF THE LONGEST days and nights Rachel had ever lived dragged by. By noon on the third day she was sure she would lose her mind if she didn't hear from either Sloan or Victoria Colby soon.

Josh had colored in his new coloring book until he'd fallen asleep in the middle of the bed. They couldn't just keep staying here cooped up like this. This was ridiculous, she decided, she should just go to Sloan. She and Josh had left their things there. Though she'd bought a few clothes to get them through, she still had a legitimate excuse to go back to Sloan's house. But she couldn't do it. If he wanted her, he would come for her. She had known that this would be the way of it. Though she felt certain Sloan had feelings for her, for Josh even, they would never have a future together. Their combined pasts were too painful. Josh was still Angel's son, there was no changing that. She had to face the facts. Sloan didn't want her or her son in his life. She couldn't make him feel something that wasn't there.

The telephone rang and Rachel lunged for it. It had to be Sloan. "Yes," she answered, breathless.

"Miss Larson?"

It wasn't Sloan.

"Yes, this is Rachel Larson."

"This is Ric Martinez from the Colby Agency."

Rachel's heart sped into overdrive. This was the investigator Victoria had assigned to check into Tanya's story.

"Do you have news?" she demanded, impatient.

"Yes ma'am, I do. But I would prefer to discuss the information in person. Could we meet?"

Rachel frowned. "Where are you?"

"In the lobby of your hotel."

"I'm in room 223."

"I'll be right up. And Mr. Ashton is with me."

Rachel placed the receiver back in its base and tried to slow her racing heart. It had to be good news. Why would Mr. Martinez and the Colby Agency attorney have come all this way otherwise? They wouldn't. Victoria would simply have called.

She opened the door on the first knock. A tall, lean man waited outside, a large envelope in his hand. As his name and accent suggested, Martinez was Latin.

He removed his designer sunglasses and tucked them into his shirt as his throat. "Miss Larson, I'm Ric Martinez." He stepped inside her door. "And this is Zach Ashton."

Rachel's gaze shifted to the man who entered her room next. Older than Martinez, late thirties maybe, Mr. Ashton looked every bit the lawyer. Despite the heat, he wore a suit, the jacket draped over his left arm, his pristine white shirt remarkably devoid of wrinkles.

"Miss Larson, it's a pleasure to meet you." Ashton offered his hand. "We have some good news for you."

Rachel pushed the door shut, then took his hand. "Did you find him?"

Ashton gave her hand a quick shake. "Yes, we did." He turned to Martinez. "Ric will bring you up to speed on the case."

Hope mushroomed inside Rachel. She wanted to shout for joy but she contained herself until she heard the rest. "Would you like to sit down?" she offered, remembering her manners.

"That's all right, ma'am, we're fine," Ric Martinez assured her. "Katrina Renaldi lives just outside Detroit with a ten-year-old boy." He withdrew a hand full of eight-by-ten glossies from the envelope he held and passed them to Rachel. "She claims legal guardianship of the boy whom she says was orphaned by a distant relative seven years ago."

Rachel stared at the pictures in her hand. The boy was tall for ten. His hair was blond, thick and slightly curly, with the same sky-blue eyes as Sloan. She had no doubt that this was his son.

"What name is he using?" she wanted to know.

"Mark Renaldi."

Mark. That was Sloan's son's name. It had to be him. "Is this enough proof?"

"Not quite," Ashton interjected. "We needed more conclusive evidence."

"Needed?" Rachel prodded.

Martinez grinned sheepishly. Rachel had to admit, when exposed to that brilliant smile, Ric Martinez was a true Latin hunk. Zach Ashton was every bit as handsome, in a more classic, sophisticated way. Rachel suddenly wondered if drop-dead gorgeous was a prerequisite for working at the Colby Agency. Sloan certainly fit the bill.

"I ran his prints, and they were a perfect match for the ones on file with missing persons for Sloan's son," Martinez explained. "It's him. There's no doubt." He gathered the pictures from her and slid them back into the envelope. "If the woman puts up a fuss, they can always do DNA testing. But I'd bet my as—" he cleared his throat "—my next paycheck that the test would confirm my findings."

Rachel frowned, confused. "How did you get the boy's prints?"

Martinez raked his fingers through his jet-black hair. "I salvaged his milk carton."

"You what?" she asked in disbelief.

Aston shook his head, a wry smile on his lips. "You don't want to know."

"I had lunch in the school cafeteria. The female attendant was very friendly," Martinez explained. "It wasn't—"

"That's okay," Rachel cut in. "I'm sure you did what you had to." Mr. Martinez appeared to use those Latin good looks to his advantage when working on a case. Victoria had been right in choosing him.

"Mrs. Colby is anxious to notify Sloan," Mr. Ashton began, "but she asked that we get word to you first. She thought you might want to tell him personally."

Rachel wasn't sure that was a good idea now. She hadn't heard from Sloan since that awful morning…with Angel. Maybe he didn't want to see her again. He'd done what she hired him to do, what else did she expect? He hadn't made any promises. *I won't hold you to any promises you make tonight.* Sloan's words echoed inside her head. They had no future together. She had known that from the beginning.

"Maybe you should tell him," Rachel suggested. "I'm not sure—"

A knock at the door interrupted her. She looked from the door to Martinez, then to Ashton. "Did someone else come with you?"

"No. Just the two of us." Martinez stopped her when she would have reached for the door. "Would you like me to answer it?" he suggested.

She shook her head. "No. I'll get it." She was through being afraid, through hiding. Angel was dead.

Rachel tamped down the foolish hope that it might be Sloan. If he had wanted to see her, he would have come already. Or maybe it would be him. After all, he hadn't collected his fee yet. For that matter, he hadn't even named an amount. Whether he wanted her or not, he would probably want his money.

"Excuse me." Drawing in a deep, steadying breath, Rachel stepped between the two men and pulled the door open. She stared up into Sloan's piercing blue eyes and her heart lurched. Unable to utter a word, she drank in the beauty of him as if it had been a lifetime since she'd seen him instead of only a couple of days.

"I was afraid you'd be gone." His gaze flicked to Martinez and Ashton then back to her. "I had an emergency that couldn't wait." He glanced at the two strangers again. Something changed in his eyes. "Is this a bad time?"

She knew better than to hope that what she saw in that translucent blue gaze was jealousy. "No." Rachel stepped back. "Please come in." She'd been so caught up in staring at him that she hadn't thought to ask him in. "This is Ric Martinez and Zach Ashton from the Colby Agency."

A line of confusion marring his brow, Sloan accepted the hand Martinez offered first, then Ashton's.

"It's an honor to meet you, man," Martinez said eagerly. "You're a legend at the agency."

A ghost of a smile twitched Sloan's lips. "A legend, huh?"

"Absolutely." Martinez was clearly impressed.

"Well after forty-eight hours of surveillance and

nonstop travel, I definitely feel old enough to be a legend.''

"Sloan, Martinez brought some news,'' Rachel told him, broaching the subject, but not quite sure how to begin.

Sloan turned back to her, his eyes full of something that looked a lot like hope. She would gladly have traded a year of her life to kiss him right then, but she had to do this first. He'd suffered too long already.

"What news?'' He looked from her to Martinez and back.

"I spoke to Tanya after her surgery,'' Rachel ventured, not sure how you told a man this sort of news. "She confirmed what Angel told you about your son.''

Sloan's expression grew wary. "What do you mean?''

"She said your son is alive.'' Rachel took the envelope containing the pictures from Martinez's hand and opened it. "Angel's sister has been raising him in Detroit.'' She passed the photographs to Sloan.

Rachel watched, holding her breath, as myriad emotions stole across Sloan's face. He looked at Rachel then, afraid to believe, but desperate for someone to make it all right.

"Martinez—'' she stopped to compose herself "—he managed to get the boy's prints. They match your son's.'' A sob caught the last word.

Sloan turned to Martinez. "How close was the match?''

"As close to perfect as you can get. The kid has to be your son. The woman suddenly shows up in a new town seven years ago with a three-year-old boy. There's no adoption papers, no history of the kid prior to that.''

"Take me to him.''

The softly uttered command was directed at Martinez.

"We can leave now," Ashton suggested. "We'll discuss the legal ramifications and steps we'll need to take en route."

Sloan nodded. "Good." He turned to Rachel. "I have to go, but I will be back."

Rachel nodded, unable to speak without losing her grip on the tidal wave of emotions looming over her.

Sloan grabbed her and kissed her. The taste of his lips sealed her fate. She would love him for the rest of her life, whether he ever loved her or not.

LATE THE NEXT afternoon Rachel and Josh left for New Orleans. She couldn't bear to stay in Mexico another day. Sloan hadn't called. She was very happy that he had found his son, but it was clear to her, that he wasn't interested in her and Josh. He had said he'd had an emergency and that's why he hadn't been to her hotel before, but he could have called. He could call now. She couldn't do this to herself any longer.

She sighed. He probably had his son back by now. What did he need with her and Josh? He had his own family. Besides, what did they really know about each other? Nothing. Two people with a connected past had reached out to each other during a time of horrendous stress, and now it was over.

Rachel had to get on with her life. It wasn't fair to Josh for her to mope around like this, and it wasn't fair to her. The fall semester would begin in a few days. Josh would be starting preschool, she might as well sign up for a few classes at the university. Her father would have wanted her to finish her education. And she had to find something to do with herself if she couldn't be with Sloan. Her heart ached at the dream that would never come true.

It was time she and Josh started a normal life. With or without Sloan. He had come to her hotel that day. Maybe he planned to tell her how he felt, but had gotten derailed with the news about his son, which was entirely understandable. Or maybe he simply wanted his fee.

Enough, Rachel, she chastised. *Time to put the past behind you.* She had Josh to think of.

Early the next morning, Rachel determined to do something about her state of depression. She dressed in the lovely print dress Sloan had bought her the day they'd gone shopping. He might never be a part of her life again, but she would never forget him. He had changed something inside her. Given her back the confidence and trust Angel had taken away. He would always be more than a hero to her.

Determined to take the first step in getting on with the rest of her life, Rachel left Josh with her neighbor, Detective Taylor's wife, and visited the nearby university campus. Though she admired the lovely campus and the offerings were extensive, she couldn't bring herself to actually sign up for anything. She gathered all the necessary forms and a schedule of what classes were offered just in case. She could look everything over tonight. Maybe then she could make a decision about what to do. There was still time.

Halfway across the deserted parking lot, Rachel stopped dead in her tracks. Sloan was leaning against her car, waiting for her. He looked wonderful. From the plain white T-shirt to the faded jeans that gloved his muscular body, he looked like the man she loved. His hair was loose, the way she liked it. He looked amazing, like some Greek god come to rescue her from the humdrum of everyday life.

Ignoring the hope soaring inside her, Rachel covered the distance that separated them with measured steps. She clutched the papers and college catalog to her chest as if she could keep him from seeing what was in her heart. But she knew she couldn't. Her love of him was shining in her eyes, she felt certain.

"Hello, Sloan." She moistened her lips. "What brings you to the Big Easy?"

His gaze lingered on her lips for a very long time before he spoke. "Unfinished business. We have some settling up to do."

Rachel blinked, taken aback. His fee. "Oh. I'm sorry. I guess you thought I'd run out on you. But you were busy and I couldn't hang around that hotel forever." She shrugged. God, she was rambling. "If you'd like to follow me to my bank I'll have a cashier's check drawn up for you."

"First, I wanted to thank you for helping find my son." He stared at the pavement for a moment. "I really believed he was dead. I wouldn't have asked Tanya." He shook his head. "I couldn't risk that much pain. I would have just spent the rest of my life believing he was gone."

"It was the least I could do." Profound relief washed over her at the confirmation that he did, indeed, have his son back. "No one should be able to take your child and get away with it."

Sloan nodded his agreement. "He's grown so much. It's hard to accept that I've missed all this time with him."

"It'll be fine," she assured him. "What about the woman, is she going to give you any trouble?"

"Actually, she's been very cooperative. She found

out a few months ago that she has terminal cancer. She had already written Mark a letter explaining everything. The letter was to be opened upon her death.'' Sloan blew out a breath. ''She's made her peace with God, now she just wants to be sure Mark is going to be okay. Despite how it sounds, I guess I'm grateful to her for swaying Angel from his original plan.''

He fell silent then.

Rachel blinked back the tears threatening to expose her turbulent feelings. ''So what happens now?''

''Since she only has a few days to live, I've agreed to let Mark stay with her until the end under my or Martinez's strict supervision. Then I'll bring him home.''

''I'm happy for you, Sloan.'' She shifted the load in her arms. ''If you'd like to go to the bank now, we'll settle up.''

''Actually, I know a little wedding chapel in Vegas where they do the kind of settling up I had in mind.''

Rachel almost dropped her load. He couldn't mean what she thought he meant.

Sloan took the papers from her. ''Your keys?'' He held out his hand.

Rachel fumbled for the keys in her purse, then passed them to him. He opened her car door and tossed the papers and the catalog onto the passenger seat. He reached for her purse and tossed it inside as well. Shoving her keys into his pants pocket he turned back to her.

He pulled her close. ''I don't know how you did it, but you got under my skin, Rachel Larson.'' He tucked a tendril of hair behind her ear. ''You blew me away. Every time I tried to push it away, the feelings just got stronger. I want to spend the rest of my life with you.''

''You're sure about that?''

He tightened his hold on her waist. "Oh, yes. Very sure."

He brushed a tender kiss across her lips.

"What about your fee?" she teased. She fiddled with the collar of his shirt, wishing she could tear it off him right now, right here, and touch that sculpted chest beneath.

"How about you pay me in installments?"

Rachel frowned petulantly. "Installments?"

He kissed that ultrasensitive place next to her ear. "Sounds like a good plan to me. I'll collect every night, maybe even every morning too."

Rachel shivered as he trailed a path of kisses along the line of her jaw. "When did you plan to start collecting?"

"Right now," he growled against her skin.

She shivered again, then drew back slightly. "What about Josh?" She held her breath. How could he ever accept Josh as his son?

Sloan looked directly into her eyes, his expression suddenly serious. "Josh will be my son too." He hesitated, then added, "If that's acceptable to you."

Tears welled in her eyes. "That's very acceptable to me." She moistened her lips, tasting the man she loved with all her heart. "I love you, Sloan."

He smiled, a gesture that squeezed her heart. "I have something for you." He fished something from his pocket, then held it between his thumb and forefinger. "Just a little something to seal the deal."

Rachel stilled, her gaze fixed on the delicate diamond ring he held so gingerly. "I don't know what to say."

He lifted her left hand and slid the ring onto her finger. "Just say yes."

She frowned, uncertain, her heart pounding so hard

she couldn't think. "But I don't have anything to give you."

He pressed his lips to her cheek, then nuzzled her neck. "How about a little girl to go with our boys," he whispered.

Rachel's heart leaped for joy. She slid her arms around his lean waist and squeezed her eyes shut. He loved her. He wanted a family with her...and with Josh. "How about two, to make it an even match," she suggested, then moaned as his tongue laved the pulse point at the base of her throat that pounded out her need for him.

"Is that a yes?" He drew back to look deeply into her eyes, his own glazed with desire.

"That's definitely a yes." She tiptoed and kissed his waiting lips.

He squeezed her buttocks, lifting her against the evidence of his need for her. "I'm a firm believer in consummating all important deals."

"There's a hotel only a couple of blocks from here," she said breathlessly. "We could be there in three minutes."

He ground her hips into his once more. "I was thinking more along the lines of your back seat and *now*."

Rachel surveyed the empty parking lot and reached behind her to open the door. "You are wicked."

He grinned. "Nobody ever accused me of being a saint."

Rachel pulled him down for another kiss. He might not be a saint, but he was her savior. And she loved him all the more for his wicked ways.

Epilogue

Victoria waited patiently for Ric Martinez to arrive at her office. She smiled. Of all the investigators she'd had the pleasure of working with, Ric had the most attitude. Though he was a fine young man, he still had a few rough edges.

Speaking of the devil, he burst into the room, looking for all the world like a Latin cover model fresh off a steamy romance novel.

"Sorry I'm late, Victoria," he offered, though she knew he was completely unrepentant. "I had a call that just wouldn't wait."

From a lady friend, no doubt. Victoria resisted the urge to shake her head. How could you fault a man who was as charming as Elvis and as sinfully handsome as the latest Latin pop performer? He simply could not help himself. And he was a damned good investigator. He had proven himself worthy more than once.

"That's not a problem, Martinez," she assured him. "I wanted you to stop by so I could go over your latest performance evaluation."

That took the starch out of his Casanova attitude. He

cleared his throat and straightened in his chair. "Performance evaluation?"

Victoria nodded. "We do those from time to time around here."

"So," he smiled that mega charming, lady-killer smile, "how'd I do?"

"Actually." Victoria shuffled the pages in front of her that had absolutely nothing to do with Ric Martinez. "You're doing rather well, the attitude not withstanding."

"I'm working on that," he said with exaggerated humility.

"I'm certain you are." Victoria tossed the papers aside. "So, with that in mind, I've decided to put you on full field operative status."

His handsome face lit up like a neon sign. "No sh—" His eyes widened at his near faux pas. He cleared his throat again. "Really? That's great."

"The next assignment I get that suits your personality and skills is yours."

He pushed to his feet, his lean body restless with anticipation. "Thanks, Victoria. I won't let you down."

"Oh, I know you won't, Martinez."

"Anything else?"

He was itching to spread the word. He had waited, somewhat impatiently, for this moment. He should savor it. Martinez had worked hard to overcome the poverty and tragedy of his youth.

"No, that's all."

Victoria watched him walk away. He opened the door and started out, then paused and shot her another of those devilish grins. She wondered if there was a woman alive that could resist the man. One thing was certain, were she twenty years younger, she surely couldn't.

Before Martinez could get away, Zach Ashton leaned in through the open doorway. "Victoria, do you and Martinez have a minute?"

"We do," Victoria answered for Martinez as well, giving him a look that stalled the protest he would have launched.

Resigned to a few more minutes in the boss's office, Martinez followed Ashton back to the two chairs flanking her desk.

"We have a bit of a problem with an informant from the Malloy case." Ashton flicked an annoyed glance at Martinez. "She says that Martinez tricked her into talking to him by telling her that he represented some *New York* magazine."

"I never actually said that," Martinez interjected quickly. "She *assumed* and I simply allowed her to do so." He cut Ashton a look. "I don't see the problem, man. I didn't promise the lady anything. I just let her do the talking."

Ashton exhaled a long-suffering breath. "The problem *is*—" he glared at Martinez for emphasis "—that now she wants to sue. Granted, she's a hooker with a rap sheet a mile long, but there will be some lowlife attorney somewhere who will be happy to represent her."

"Hey, man, what can I say?" Martinez shrugged. "I do what I have to do to get the job done." He inclined his head, returning Ashton's less than sympathetic gaze. "Now, I guess you have to do yours."

Victoria couldn't suppress the smile that twitched her lips. The two men were so totally opposite, they went head-to-head often. Martinez with his streetwise attitude and cockiness, refused to conform. He could talk a desert dweller into buying sand, his manner of dress every bit as slick and cutting edge as his persuasion skills. Victoria's gaze shifted to Ashton, the personification of the educated, refined gentleman. Ashton played by the rules. And he was one of the top ten attorneys in the nation.

"I don't think you quite understand my point, Martinez," Ashton was saying.

Before either could build up a full head of steam Victoria spoke, "Put in a call to Carlton Hughes at the *Journal*," she instructed Ashton. "He owes me a favor. Let the young lady have her interview." Victoria studied the two handsome faces before her, Martinez's expectant, Ashton's simply tolerant. "Never let it be said that the Colby Agency doesn't follow through on its promises."

"I'll take care of it." Ashton stood. He cast one last cross look at Martinez. "Since I don't have anything else to do at the moment."

Martinez pushed to his feet. "Hey, man—" he followed Ashton to the door, "—just think how boring your job would be without me."

Victoria watched the two men exit her office, Martinez offering to buy Ashton's lunch, Ashton graciously refusing. No matter how much each man went against the grain of the other, the respect was there, however well concealed. Victoria was extremely lucky to have both on her staff, keeping the Colby Agency the best in the business.

Don't miss Ric Martinez's story in
PERSONAL PROTECTOR,
the next COLBY AGENCY *story*
by Debra Webb
on sale April 2002.

Prologue

"I hope you're not leaving out anything relevant, Lucas." Victoria leveled her gaze on her oldest and dearest friend. That sprinkling of gray at his temples and the sparkle in those devilish gray eyes wreaked havoc with her usual strict control.

Lucas's smile widened at the implication. "Don't you trust me, Victoria?" He propped his cane against the arm of his chair and tilted his head, emphasizing his question. A hint of amusement flickered in his eyes.

In blatant skepticism, Victoria arched one eyebrow a fraction higher than the other. "I don't trust anyone who has worked for the *Company* and Special Ops as long as you have."

"Well," he offered in that smoky voice that did strange things to her ability to think rationally, "I suppose I can't blame you there. But you know I would never deceive you, Victoria."

The sound of her name on his lips sent a rush of warmth through her. Yes, she knew he was telling the truth. Lucas would never do anything to hurt her. He had always been there for her, and now she would have one of those rare opportunities to repay him just a little of what she owed.

"All right, then, I believe I have the perfect man for the job." Victoria pressed the intercom button. "Mildred, please ask Ric Martinez to join this meeting."

"Martinez?" Lucas frowned. "I don't think I know him."

"He's fairly new," Victoria agreed. "But he's good. And he has the right background for the job."

"Mind if I perform a little screening test of my own?" All signs of amusement had vanished from his expression. "After all, this is my one and only niece we're talking about."

Victoria shrugged lightly. "Be my guest."

The door opened and Ric Martinez stepped inside the room. Tall, dark and handsome, the man's Latin good looks combined with his fountain of charm proved valuable assets in this business. Ric Martinez could charm or con anything out of anyone.

Ric's gaze darted from Victoria to Lucas and back. "You wanted to see me," he said as he closed the door behind him.

"Yes. Please have a seat." She gestured to the vacant chair in front of her desk. Before Ric could sit, Lucas made his move.

"Close your eyes, Martinez." Lucas stood next to Ric now, the barrel of his weapon pressed to the younger man's temple. Despite his physical handicap, Lucas could still move with more stealth than most when it served his purpose.

Ric's gaze, still locked on Victoria, widened, then narrowed with suspicion. "What's going on, man?" he demanded uncertainly.

"Close your eyes," Lucas snapped.

Victoria gave Ric a nod and he immediately complied. She had no idea what Lucas had in mind, but whatever it was, it would be harmless, yet prove immensely telling.

"Okay, man," Ric said stiffly. "Just stay cool."

"Oh, I'm cool, Martinez." The tip of the weapon bored a little deeper into Ric's skull. "The question is, are you?"

"I'm anything you need me to be."

"What did you see when you walked into this room?"

His eyes still closed tight, Ric frowned. "What?"

"Give your boss a profile on the man who might just blow your brains out in the next thirty seconds."

"Black hair, with a bit of gray," Ric began, his posture considerably more relaxed now that he had an idea what was expected of him. "Fairly tall, lean build. Fifty years old, maybe." His brow creased in thought. "You have a small scar on your cheek just beneath your right eye. And you obviously use a cane."

"Anything else?" Lucas barked impatiently.

"Oh, yeah," Ric continued, in that cocky tone that set him apart from Victoria's other investigators. "You're wearing a knockoff watch, a cheap navy blue suit and loafers just like my *abuelo* used to wear."

Victoria watched the smile inch its way across Lucas's grim mouth. She smiled, as well. Lucas was definitely one of a kind. And so was Ric Martinez, the grandfather remark not withstanding.

"All right, Martinez." Lucas lowered his weapon. "You can have a seat now." Lucas's smile widened to a grin when Ric's annoyed gaze connected with his. "Unless, of course, you need to go change your shorts."

"I'm cool," Ric said, grinding the words out as he took the seat she had offered earlier.

"You're right, Victoria." Lucas settled back into his own chair. "He is good."

"Does anyone mind letting me in on the joke?" Ric demanded, irritation clear in his tone. "I knew there was a certain level of risk involved when I signed on," he said pointedly as he pinned Victoria with that dark gaze. "I just didn't expect to find it in your office."

Victoria reined in her smile and adopted a more businesslike expression. "Ric, this is Lucas Camp. He's with a highly covert special ops organization of which I'm not at liberty to discuss. And he's a very dear friend of mine." Disbelief clouded the younger man's eyes briefly. He probably wondered how she knew a man like Lucas. She knew a great many things that Ric was entirely too new in this business to even fathom.

Ric felt certain he wouldn't soon forget this meeting. Just who the hell was this guy anyway? Ric shifted his gaze to the man who had held a gun to his head only moments before. Despite his lingering uneasiness, Ric leaned forward and extended his hand. "I would say that it's a pleasure, Mr. Camp, but I wouldn't want to lie."

Lucas shook Ric's hand firmly. "If you'd said it was, I'd have to change my opinion of you."

"Ric, I have an assignment that I feel you are particularly suited for," Victoria said, drawing his attention back to her and away from the man who had seriously annoyed him.

Ric straightened in his chair. Maybe he was finally going to get a real assignment. "That's great," he said with a new sense of anticipation. It was well past time that Victoria recognized his potential.

She passed a manila folder to him. "This is Piper

Ryan,'' Victoria explained. ''She's a new correspondent for WYBN-TV in Atlanta.''

Ric opened the folder as he listened. His gaze instantly riveted to the glossy head shot of a young and extraordinarily beautiful woman. ''Whoa! This is one hot number.''

''Piper is Lucas's niece,'' Victoria added pointedly.

Ric's gut clenched. *Damn.* He lifted his gaze to meet the death-ray Lucas aimed in his direction. ''I meant beautiful in a sisterly kind of way.''

Lucas's intense gaze cut to Victoria. ''And you're certain he's the best man for the job?''

Ric tensed. *Damn.* His first big chance and he screws up by sticking his big foot in his mouth.

''Quite certain,'' Victoria affirmed.

Relief rushed through him. Maybe he hadn't stepped too far out of line. ''What's the deal with Pi—Miss Ryan?'' he inquired, doing his level best to ignore the daggers still emanating from Lucas's deadly glare.

''One month ago Piper and five other reporters were invited to a secret press conference for a terrorist group called the Soldiers of the Sovereign Union, or SSU.''

Ric nodded. Though he hadn't seen Piper on the news, he had watched some of the highly publicized results of the secret press conference. He remembered that the reporters had been blindfolded and taken to some remote location. The leader of the group had hoped to garner sympathy in the press. But what they had reported in the media was anything but sympathetic to the terrorist's cause.

''I saw a couple of the news reports,'' he told Victoria.

''Then you know that to date three of the reporters have died violent deaths at the hands of these people.

The FBI is investigating and is providing protection for the remaining reporters, including Piper.'' Victoria's gaze darted to Lucas.

"What role will I be playing?"

"Lucas is going to coordinate part of that setup," Victoria told him. "With your videographer expertise, I'm certain you will fit right in as Piper's new cameraman. Your assignment will be to shadow her every step."

"What about after work hours?"

"I've taken care of that, too," Lucas answered this time. "I arranged for Piper's next-door neighbor to win a two-week vacation to Hawaii. He left today. You'll be apartment-sitting, so to speak, while he's vacationing."

Ric cocked his eyebrow. "And your niece won't be suspicious of my sudden appearance in both her professional as well as her personal life?"

Lucas met Ric's questioning gaze. "My niece is a very busy young woman. She won't waste time wondering anything about you."

Ignoring the blatant attempt to take him down a couple of notches, Ric smiled politely. "Good." He rubbed at his chin a moment, his gaze lingering on the older man's. "It does seem rather strange to me though that you don't trust the FBI to take care of your niece. Any particular reason?"

Victoria cleared her throat in warning. He was pushing it here.

"I didn't survive so long in this business without taking extra precautions, Martinez. I never leave anything to chance."

"Does the FBI have anyone inside?" Ric asked, effectively moving past the nerve he had obviously just hit.

"They have a man in the SSU." Lucas propped his hand on his cane. "And I have someone special waiting to provide you with any backup you may require."

"Jack Raine has come out of retirement," Victoria added for clarification. "He's the best there is. You can count on him." She glanced at Lucas. "Though I am surprised you talked him into taking time away from his wife and new son."

Ric remembered Jack Raine well. His case was legendary around here.

"The bottom line, Martinez," Lucas interjected, "is that I want someone watching my niece who has no political stake in any of this." He shifted in his chair, looking directly at Ric now. "I want you to eat, sleep and breathe Piper Ryan until I can stop these bastards."

"I can do that," Ric assured him.

"I hope so, Martinez." Lucas leveled a warning gaze on him. "Because I'm counting on you *personally* to keep my niece safe. Don't let me down."

Ric met his lethal glare. "Trust me, Mr. Camp. Keeping Piper Ryan safe will be a walk in the park."

COMING SOON FROM
HARLEQUIN®
INTRIGUE®
AND
CASSIE MILES

Two exciting titles in a new miniseries!

When it comes to saving lives, these brave heroes and heroines show no fear. Join them for edge-of-your-seat suspense and, as always, happily-ever-after romance.

STATE OF EMERGENCY
On sale January 2002

WEDDING CAPTIVES
On sale February 2002

Available at your favorite retail outlet.

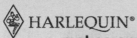

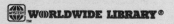

TRUEBLOOD, TEXAS

Coming in February 2002...

HOT ON HIS TRAIL
by
Karen Hughes

Lost:

Her so-called life. After being sheltered by her mother for years, Calley Graham hopes to sign on as a full-time investigator for Finders Keepers.

Found:

One tough trail boss. Matt Radcliffe doesn't have time during his cattle drive for a pesky investigator who insists on dragging him back to Pinto, Texas.

But Calley is one determined woman—so she volunteers as camp cook on Matt's drive, hoping to keep her job...and maybe the cowboy, too!

Finders Keepers: bringing families together

HARLEQUIN®
Makes any time special ®

Visit us at www.eHarlequin.com

TBTCNM6